HELLHOUND ON MY TRAIL

ROCK BAND FIGHTS EVIL #1

HELLHOUND ON MY TRAIL

ROCK BAND FIGHTS EVIL #1

D.J. Butler

WordFire Press
Colorado Springs, Colorado

CHAPTER ONE

Wah wah, ch-ch-chang! The guitar crunched out the end of the chorus with a cymbal crash.

Across the room, the bouncer of Butcher's looked like he was having a bad night. He leaned against the slightly lopsided bar and scanned the thin crowd with contempt, arms crossed over his denim jacket and a semi-automatic pistol visible in his belt. He shook his scarred, buzz-cut head every minute or so like he was trying to knock the sound of the music out.

Mike didn't care what the bouncer thought of the music. He hadn't seen his brother's ghost all day, and he needed a drink to keep things that way. The only reason Mike even noticed the bouncer was that the man was between him and the alcohol. The booze would keep his brother at bay for a little while. Also, after the set, Mike planned to shoot himself, and he preferred to die drunk.

Mike launched into the break, his memory guiding him through the changes. He'd arrived minutes before the show and Eddie had barked at him through the first part of the set, scrawling some notes on a greasy paper bag. It had been enough. After getting his marching orders, Mike had headed straight for the bar—and Eddie had corralled him back onto the stage before he could get his hands on even so much as a warm beer.

The drummer rode with Mike into the break while everyone else fell quiet. *Twitch*, that was the drummer's name, and he hit the skins with a light touch, but perfect timing. Mike nodded and grinned at Twitch and he grinned back as they held down the groove together, Mike boogying with a chromatic run that was probably more jazz than this shabby little blues-rock band was used to, up to the fifth over and over. Maybe he was showing off, just a bit, but it was his last gig. Ever.

The drum kit was a little minimalist, just a kick, snare, one tom, and a high hat. The drummer played with thick sticks that looked more like cudgels than something you'd buy at Guitar Barn. Twitch wore shiny black leathers from head to foot, the kind with studs in all the impossible places, so that he looked like some kind of black and silver sex porcupine. Mike thought of him as a guy, but actually, looking at the drummer now, he wasn't so sure. Twitch could have been a woman with a slightly strong jaw line or a man with a thin nose and eyebrows. Man or woman, the worst thing about Twitch's get-up was that it had a tail, a full horse's tail, silver-colored like the drummer's own long hair, that came right out of Twitch's backside and brushed the floor as he drummed. Twitch looked like he'd whip you, if you paid him.

Then Eddie jumped in, workmanlike power chords chomping over the beat, with the occasional blues flourish curling in the treble. Eddie was a slight black man with short curly hair, in a green military-style jacket with lots of pockets and jeans that had too many holes for any thrift store to take them. Mike had played with lots of guitarists who swanned and clowned and danced, but Eddie shrank back from the edge of the stage. He huddled over his instrument and carefully watched his fingering, which was good, because his playing was okay, at best. The axe Eddie worked on was a crummy red Toronado, a Fender like Mike's P-Bass, but made in Mexico. And discontinued, he thought, because nobody wanted to buy the things. It was red and worn to the wood where Eddie's forearm rubbed it, but the sound, running through a small bank of pedals at Eddie's feet, was crisp.

Eddie had some kind of manager role, too. It had been Eddie who had called him that morning, woken him from a scratchy, uncomfortable sleep into throbbing, painful wakefulness. Eddie had said he'd gotten Mike's card off the bulletin board in a guitar shop in San Antonio, and that there was gig for him tonight, if he could find a crappy little bar outside a crappy little town that wasn't on most maps, on a road that might or might not be indicated as a lumber trail. Bass and amp could both be provided.

That was good, because Mike's amp was in hock.

The crowd mostly ignored Eddie. Hard roadside drinkers that they were, they kept to their seats under the buzzing fluorescent tubes nailed to two-by-fours undergirding the tin-sheet ceiling, sucked their beer and spirits and watched Jim—the singer—like at any moment he might collapse to the floor or take flight. Some of them sent shots up to fortify or reward him, which made Mike lick his lips in anticipation of the first break.

Except there was this one guy, at the little round table nearest the stage, who stared at Eddie the whole time. He was a short guy in a polo shirt and a sport coat and a straw Panama hat, and his shoes were way too shiny for rural New Mexico. He gripped the little table with both hands like he had fallen off the *Titanic* and it was his raft, and he talked the whole time, though he was alone. After staring at the guy long enough, Mike thought he could read his lips. *Tambourine,* he was saying. *Tambourine, Mr. Marlowe, please play the Tambourine.* His face shone with sweat, though Butcher's was, if anything, a little cool.

Marlowe was Eddie's name, Mike remembered. Eddie didn't have a tambourine, he didn't look at the guy who stared at him, and as Mike looked at Eddie, the guitar player spat on the floor.

Then the organ player piled in like a Mac truck. He was loud and had a big sound, like he was playing with all ten fingers and both feet simultaneously, but Mike thought he could hear dropped notes, and the guy's timing was off. Adrian was short and square and dressed in something that looked like a sharkskin suit, but much cheaper. He was dwarfed by his Hammond electric organ, with upper and lower manuals. Other electronic gadgets were piled up around the Hammond, effects pedals and a MIDI controller and a drum machine and other stuff that Mike didn't recognize. Mike was strictly a bass man, really, and didn't go in for toys.

Adrian hit the big climax, flatted sevenths blaring like a rock-and-roll thumb in the eye, and then Jim jumped in with the last choruses.

"Keep your head down," Jim sang.
"Sleep between shows, and watch out
For the punches love throws!"

Jim's voice boomed and echoed surprisingly loud in the small bar. It sounded like it had reverb in it, but Mike couldn't figure out where that might be coming from. It wasn't the mic—that was a plain vanilla SM58, standard issue for bar bands the world over. Mike didn't think it could be the PA, either; he'd watched Harry the bartender set the faders before the show started and then shuffle back behind the bar, and no one had touched the PA system since. The mixer was some eight-channel piece of junk from Malaysia, anyway.

Jim was a tall, broad-shouldered Viking, with long black hair and the kind of pale skin that you got if you never went out in the sun. He looked so rugged and handsome in his long white prairie-style shirt and blue jeans, even Mike noticed, and he was not a man who looked at other men. Women probably loved Jim, Mike thought bitterly. He probably had no trouble at all with the ladies.

Mike amped up the last chorus with the rest of the band, picking up the tempo slightly and then sustaining as Jim belted out the last lines—

"Keeps your eyes on the waves, boy,
Thar she blows!
And watch out for the punches love throws!—"

and then Mike dove into one last round of tonic-sub-dominant-tonic to close out the song, hammering on all cylinders with the rest of the band. He hit his last note short and sweet, then stepped back and ignored the hoots and applause of the crowd, gripping his lovingly polished P-Bass with both hands and staring at the bar.

Butcher's was a real dive, a roadhouse made of concrete with the rebar showing in middle of nowhere, and had a crowd to suit it. Neon spangled the plywood over the bar, advertising mostly low-end beer and tequila, though there was a glowing Bacardi clock in the middle of it all, to add a little class and to warn the drinkers when closing hour drew near. Mostly the place smelled of sour alcohol and cold air breathed way too many times, but there was a distinct note of piss buried in the stink. Mike hoped it was just because the stage was too close to the restroom.

He was a little bummed to be about to shoot himself in a place that reeked, but not bummed enough to make him change his plans. The gun was in his Impala in the parking lot, anyway. He could just shoot himself out there, or get nice and hammered and walk out into the sand somewhere where no one would notice and the coyotes would eat his body.

In the rowdy crowd were truckers in baseball caps and flannel shirts, Indians wearing cowboy hats from the reservation Mike dimly knew was out in the hills somewhere north of the bar, Mexicans, and two or three hard-bitten, sand-blasted people who might have been local ranchers or farmers, or whatever it was people did to make a living out here in Hell-and-Gone, New Mexico. They were clapping with at least half a heart now, and a slab-faced woman with forearms like whole hams sent another beer up to Jim.

Mike sighed.

His vision swam, just a little. He needed a drink. After years of boozing to keep his brother away, he needed the alcohol not only for Chuy, but for himself, too. He hadn't had a drink since that morning. His throat itched and his belly hurt and he was sweating like a pig in a parka, though the bar was only warmed by a couple of battered space heaters in the corners. He badly wanted to open up a bottle of Jack Daniels.

The bouncer caught Mike's gaze and snarled at him.

Or, Mike thought, he could just go out into the parking lot and shoot himself sober.

It was hard to be sure, because of the tangle of neon that hung there anyway, announcing Miller Light and Budweiser and Jack Daniels and Jim Beam, but Mike thought there was something red and flashing, hanging over the bar. He was pretty certain that, whatever it was, he hadn't seen it there before.

Red and flashing and pouring out smoke.

"Is that a fire?" he stepped sideways and muttered out of the corner of his mouth to Adrian, the guy at the organ, just loud enough for the rhythm section to hear over the buzz of the crowd and Eddie's first choppy chords for the next song. His mouth felt like sandpaper as he spoke.

Adrian shrugged and scowled. "I wouldn't know, there's a light in my face. The blind leading the blind, et cetera."

Mike looked at Twitch; the drummer made a pouty face and air-kissed Mike. Mike tried to smile back, but he was pretty sure it came out as a grimace.

Eddie shambled half a step forward, chunking out a basic rock riff that he half-muted with the palm of his right hand.

"Tambourine!" Shiny Shoes bellowed from the front row. "Please!"

"This next song is called 'Falling Rocks,'" Eddie announced gruffly over his chords. Jim stared at his guitarist while he made the announcement and said nothing; Mike wondered why the singer didn't announce the song himself. "It doesn't have a tambourine in it."

"Key of *G*," Adrian reminded Mike as Eddie squeezed out the first gnarled riff.

"I remember," Mike said. "Also, I'm not deaf."

The bar exploded into red light and fire.

"Duck!" Eddie yelled, and then he and Jim threw themselves left and right, clearing the path between Mike and the lights—

and the *thing* that burst out of the red smear in the air, crashing onto the floor in an explosion of flame. The creature landed front legs first—it was built like a lion in size and shape, but smoke and fire, red and blue and black, licked up from its scaly skin—onto a table beside the bar and shattered it instantly into toothpicks. Drinkers flailed backwards, shouting and spilling their glasses.

The thing snapped open enormous jaws and let out a bellow like a police siren and a train wreck mixed together and over-driven into snarling distortion. Mike felt his own jaw drop open.

The beast swung its head and sent two more tables flying across the room. A man in a checked and yoked shirt with pearl buttons shrieked like a little girl as his shirt burst into flame on contact with the creature's snout.

Mike couldn't think, and he couldn't look away. He stared.

The bouncer lurched into the center of the room, pulling his pistol. The man was brave, anyway. Maybe his buzz cut meant he used to be a Marine or something. He fired, *bang! bang! bang!* and the creature took no notice. Its head, like a dog's, but hairless and scaly, wreathed in multi-colored flame, snapped open. Its jaws were too long, Mike noticed, transfixed and unable to look away. They were like the jaws of a crocodile.

They snapped on the bouncer's neck and decapitated him in a single swift *munch*.

The switchblade in Mike's pocket had never felt more useless.

Mike finally found his voice again. *"Mierda!"* he shouted.

"Get down!" Adrian shouted, and then a spray of bullets snapped past Mike. He threw himself sideways and found Eddie grabbing him by the front of his cracked leather jacket, dragging him off the stage to one side. A gout of flame ripped through the air behind him, singeing the back of his neck.

Mike struggled to break free, out of reflex more than anything else. Eddie knocked his hands aside like he was a child, though Mike had six inches and easily a hundred pounds on the guy, and slapped his face. "Get out of here!" the black guitarist shouted, and shoved Mike off the stage, through the swinging door under the tilted sign that read *PISSOIR*.

The last thing Mike saw before the hallway door swung shut again was Adrian, standing at his Hammond and holding something that looked no bigger than a pistol, but had a really long clip and was firing like a machine gun. And for a split second, he thought he could make out Jim, *somersaulting* forward off the front of the stage with a *sword* in his hand. He looked like Errol Flynn in the old black and white movies, if Flynn were six-and-a-half feet tall and had rock-and-roll hair.

"Die, beasty!" Adrian howled, and then Mike was alone in the hall, with a bathroom door, a payphone missing its handset, and the mixed stink of roadhouse piss and his own fearful sweat.

He staggered to lean against the wall, needing the feel of the cold concrete against his forehead and the solidity of the wall under his arm. The concrete was real. He clutched at the knot of charms around his neck—a cross that had meant a lot to his grandfather, a rabbit's foot, an ankh—he knew it was all junk, it had never helped him before, but it made him feel better to touch it. He pulled out the switchblade and flicked it open. The knife was useless—he'd stabbed other people more than once as a kid, but he knew it wouldn't do anything to the monster rampaging in the bar, and he knew that he didn't have the guts to slit his own throat with it, either.

Then he threw up, all over his own shoes. The gas station tuna sandwich tasted on its way up exactly like it had tasted on its way down, Mike thought, his mind still reeling, no better or worse.

He could hear the rattle of gunfire in the bar, and an enormous animal howling, something like a lion's only more throaty, like the creature had a saw blade in his vocal cords or was a chain smoker. He wiped sweat from his eyes and blinked at the hall he was standing in, looking for an exit.

Chuy stood there. Grinning.

"You gonna knife me, *cabrón?*" Chuy asked. He had Grandpa Archuleta's smile, and like Mike, he'd learned to curse from the old man, chewing tobacco out in the weeds behind the trailer in between long hauls in his big rig. What Chuy had that Grandpa Archuleta didn't, which had broken Grandpa's heart when he had dragged Mike down to the city morgue and forced Mike to help him identify the body, was all the wounds.

Chuy's scalp, long black hair still attached, hung open like a flap covering a pocket, exposing the bloody skull beneath. Blood ran down from the scalp and the flesh around it, but quickly became indistinguishable from all the rest of Chuy's blood. He'd been cut everywhere, not stabbed or slashed but *carved* artfully, like he'd been tattooed or even simply *written on* from head to toe by someone who was an artist. Chuy's throat had been slit—that was the last cut, the police had said, the one that had finally put him out of his misery— all the way to the spinal cord. Every cut bled, and Mike would have sworn he could smell the reek of Chuy's ghostly blood.

It was the stink of guilt.

"No," Mike said weakly. He really wanted a drink.

"Is that how you treat family, Mikey?" When he spoke, blood spilled from Chuy's lips, too. "I mean, you went and left mom alone, now you gonna knife me? Is that what you meant, with all that bullshit about being a man?"

Chuy hadn't aged, after all these years. He still looked sixteen years old, under all the blood.

Mike tried to ignore his brother, though both his hands trembled with the adrenalin and he felt like throwing up again. He wiped sweat out of his eyes again and examined the hallway—no exit, unless maybe the john had a window.

"What, you don't want to talk to me? You feeling guilty, *pendejo?* Maybe what you need is a *woman*, huh? Well, hey, brothers gotta help each other, don't they? When I needed a woman, you got me one … I think I still know where to find her!"

Horrified at the thought of what Chuy might produce next, Mike fled from his brother's ghost, heart racing. He slammed back into the chaos of the bar, elbow first and knife at his hip, ready to jump up and into the belly of anyone getting in his way. Except Chuy, of course. Mike had tried attacking his brother's ghost once, years ago, and the only effect had been to make Chuy even angrier.

Butcher's was on fire. Smoke filled the upper half of the room, so Mike coughed and bent over to run. His gut got in the way, and his lack of stamina, but fear propelled him and he scuttled as fast as he could.

He was so afraid, he didn't even try to grab his bass.

He was halfway to the door, the only exit he knew of, when a new eruption of gunfire and a sheet of flame that spun sideways across the room in front of him forced him back. In the confusion, he lost his grip on the knife and dropped it. He stumbled on something, and when he looked down he saw that it was the bouncer's headless body, jeans jacket scorched to a charcoal gray color.

"Huevos," Mike muttered, but the bouncer had a pistol. Mike picked up the gun. Five seconds of fumbling through the dead guy's pockets were rewarded with a second clip.

The gun was nothing fancy, a simple, straightforward semi-auto, the kind of pistol that cops and guys in the army carried. Mike felt reassured by the weight of the pistol in his hand, though he was no soldier. He gnashed his teeth to bite back a flood of bad memories: gangbanging and robberies and worse.

Poor Chuy.

The lizard-lion barreled across the room in front of Mike. As it reared back, its skull smashed out pieces of the ceiling, bringing a rain of flaming timbers and smoking sheets of corrugated tin. Plunging forward, claws the size of microwave ovens cracked and gouged the concrete into hot gravel. It paid Mike absolutely no attention, but the lash of its long tail—a tail that, Mike now saw, was forked at its tip—nearly knocked him over. Crocodile jaws snapped and fire jetted from its nostrils and it chomped at the singer, Jim. Jim retreated slowly, his white face whiter with fury.

And he fought it back with a sword. With his free hand Jim snatched a bottle off a table as he passed and hurled it at the monster. He retreated over a chair, rising to the top of the chair back to stab down at the creature's face and then tipping heel-first gracefully to the ground, to then hook the toe of his boot into the ladder of the chair's back and snap-kick it into the lizard-like face.

Mike would have laughed, if he hadn't felt sick, exhausted, hurt, suffocated, and afraid of burning to death. The big singer wielded a long, slender sword, like a French or Italian fencing weapon, not that Mike was really in a position to know. He wasn't a sword guy. But it wasn't the big two-handed sword, or better still, axe, that Mike would have guessed based on the guy's build and complexion, and his fighting wasn't hack and slash.

It was dancing. The lizard-lion lunged and snapped, aiming for one of Jim's legs and then the other, and the tall guy stepped neatly back and aside each time, tipping away the beast's head with the hilt of his sword, which was wrapped in a fancy steel basket, or poking it back with the point.

He almost looked like he was having fun.

Except that whenever he stabbed the creature, which happened over and over again, the point skidded off the beast's skin without leaving a mark.

The beast was between Mike and the door, blocking his escape. He raised the pistol, thumbed off the safety and squeezed the trigger. No silly turning the gun sideways to show off now, he just aimed for the big monster's chest and emptied the clip, *bang! bang! bang! bang! bang!*

Actual *sparks* flashed off the creature's hide where he'd hit it.

The creature drew back from Jim and turned to stare balefully at Mike. Its eyes were black and glassy but seemed to dance with flame, and the smoke and fire wisping off its body made it look like the hottest burner in a barbecue. Only moving, and angry.

Jim lunged to the attack once more, stabbing at the flesh around the lizard-lion's black eyes. The thing roared again and turned back to Jim, lunging in a threshing hurricane of long, smoking teeth.

"You can't stay here!" Mike heard yelling in his ear and a hand clutched his elbow. He recognized the voice as belonging to Twitch, the drummer, so he turned to look at the guy—

but there was no Twitch. Instead, a smallish white horse or a pony—Mike didn't really know the difference—stood beside him. The creature had Twitch's coloring, though, and his long silver hair. Mike grabbed the charms around his neck and wondered....

But no, that was crazy. Twitch wasn't a horse. Then the animal tapped one of its front hooves on the concrete floor and held its head low, keeping its mane out of the flames that engulfed the bar's ceiling, and then it lowered its front shoulders, almost like it was bowing to Mike before a dance.

Or inviting him to climb on.

Mike hesitated a moment, and then laughed himself out of it. "Why not?" he asked, coughing from the smoke. Weirder things had happened to him. "Jeez," he dragged himself onto the horse's back, a clumsy and awkward assault for which the animal held perfectly still, "weirder things have happened to me *tonight*."

Besides, after the grisly spectacle of Chuy's ghost and the terrifying force of nature that was the lizard-lion, the white horse looked more ridiculous than anything else, and positively benign.

Mike still wanted a drink.

The white horse plunged forward into the curtain of fire, just before a chunk of the roof collapsed in fiery ruination, shattering into sparks and charcoal on the floor. Mike wrapped his arms around the animal's neck to keep from being thrown off on its second jump, through another sheet of flame, and then he could see the door. It gaped ahead of him like a black spot in a wall of orange and red, and the horse raced for it.

Someone stepped into the door. The horse reared up, like it might attack the person, but then it dropped back onto all fours and galloped past. Mike saw that the person who'd almost gotten himself trampled was Adrian, his suit all singed and tarnished from the smoke.

The horse broke into the cold night air and Mike sucked oxygen into his lungs, coughing as the good air fought with the smoke for possession of the territory. Just as he finally felt he could breathe again, the horse bucked and he fell off, crashing to the gravel strip that served the roadhouse as a parking lot.

Whoosh! All the air immediately left his lungs again and he gasped.

Mike stared up at the sky, seeing the glittering brilliance of the desert at night and a yellowish moon squinting suspiciously over a dark sandstone butte. He heard screaming, the squealing of tires and the sputter of aged car engines as the bar's patrons fled in terror. By the time he could breathe and rolled to his feet again, the horse was gone.

Adrian stood in the doorway of the flaming roadhouse. His guns were put away and he had both his arms raised, like he was saying some kind of prayer. Eddie burst out of the flames first, racing full-tilt past Adrian and toward Mike. Mike almost turned to run, but realized he was standing next to the only car in the parking lot besides Mike's own dented Impala, a big old Dodge van with a bumper sticker reading *I BREAK FOR LAMIAE*, and instead he stepped out of the way.

Eddie jerked the van door open and started rummaging inside for something.

The beast bellowed from inside the inferno. It isn't over, Mike realized, and fumbled to switch the full clip into the pistol.

Twitch rushed out of the smoke and fire next, and Jim ran with him, half-leaning on the shoulder of the much smaller man. That's where the drummer was, Mike thought, and dismissed his silly thoughts of people changing into horses with an ironic snort. Jim still held onto his sword, and as they cleared the door, Jim peeled away, staggering and almost falling, but keeping his feet and bringing his blade up into an *en garde* position, like a Viking Zorro.

ROAR!

Mike raised the pistol.

More of the roof collapsed, sending sparks and flames higher into the silvery darkness of the night.

"Come on!" Eddie shouted, inside the van. "Where are you?"

In the fire, Mike saw movement, and the creature crawled forward. It moved slower now; maybe Jim had wounded it. Maybe *he* had wounded it, he thought, and felt a little pride at the idea.

"Now!" Twitch yelled, but he and Jim didn't move out of the way and Mike didn't have a clear shot at the thing advancing out of the flames.

Adrian shouted something that Mike couldn't understand and waved his hands in front of his face—

and collapsed to the gravel.

"Chingado."

Chapter Two

"You're Eddie Marlowe, aren't you?"

"Get away from me, man!" Eddie yelled.

Mike heard the words in one ear and tried to ignore them, focusing on the blazing pyre that had once been Butcher's roadhouse.

Jim jumped into the door of the inferno and slashed at the lizard with his sword, driving it back again into the fire. Twitch slapped at Adrian's face with the back of his hand and tapped him on the forehead with his club-like drumstick, and they were all in the way of Mike's shot. For a split second, Mike thought about just shooting himself then and there. But he was too rattled from seeing Chuy and from the other strange events of the evening, and not nearly drunk enough, so instead he turned to see what was happening at the van.

It was Shiny Shoes. The shoes weren't so shiny any more, and he was scorched from head to foot. He held his hat in his hand, burnt black, and he looked like he was begging. Firelight danced in the high sheen of sweat all over his head, making him look feverish and fanatical.

"Please, Mr. Marlowe, I know it's you. I've seen videos, and I know what you can do. I'm here, look, I'm here even with all *this*—" he gestured at the burning building. "Doesn't that tell you something?"

"It tells me you're crazy," Eddie muttered. "Get the hell outta here."

Mike had to agree with Eddie. With all the insane, impossible things happening tonight, the absolute craziest might just be this guy who stuck around through it all so he could talk to Eddie. What on earth could the guy be thinking? Irritating *maricón*.

"I want to sign you, Mr. Marlowe, I'm an agent. I can book you with the Rolling Stones tomorrow."

Even crazier. Mike shook his head.

The lizard howled again. The sound made Mike's hair stand on end, and his stomach churned like he might throw up again. He didn't know what Eddie was doing, he couldn't help Adrian, he couldn't get at the beast without running past Jim into the fire. He was helpless.

Eddie dove with both hands into a dog-eared cardboard box, rummaging. "I didn't send video to any agents," he complained.

"You didn't have to," Shiny Shoes said, sweating. "Some kid filmed you in Montreal last summer, when you did *Flight of the Bumblebee* on tambourine. They put the clip of you on YouTube."

"Damn Internet!" Eddie gruffed.

"Look, I—"

ROAR!

Whatever it was Eddie Marlowe was trying to do, Shiny Shoes the agent was getting in his way. Mike stepped forward and slapped the pistol against Shiny Shoes's forehead. "The man said *no!*" he yelled.

Shiny Shoes dropped his hat and stared up at the barrel of the pistol, which made him look cross-eyed. "Are … are you signed with someone else?" he ventured.

"Yes!" Eddie shouted. Only his feet stuck out of the Dodge door now. "Go away!"

"Wh-who?"

Mike pointed his pistol at the sky and fired off a round. "He's signed with *me!*" he shouted, and then poked Shiny Shoes in the cheek with the smoking muzzle.

"Ouch," Shiny Shoes whined, and started to back away.

ROAR!

Mike risked a look over his shoulder. Twitch was dragging Adrian to his feet, but the organist lay as limp as a stringless marionette.

"Got it!" Eddie scooted out of the van, holding up a bandolier—

hung like a cluster of grapes with hand grenades.

Shiny Shoes turned to run. "You haven't heard the last of me!" he called. "I'm not giving up on you, Mr. Marlowe! I'll be back!"

Mike watched the would-be manager run, and movement caught his eye. In the sky, over Shiny Shoes's head. Something shimmering and metallic, but moving through the air. It was like someone was out flying remote control toy airplanes, Mike thought, in the middle of the night on a deserted New Mexico highway.

"Fire in the hole!" he heard Eddie shout behind him as Shiny Shoes disappeared, and then he remembered.

"My bass!" Mike shouted, and wheeled around. Eddie lobbed a grenade neatly over Adrian and Twitch, bouncing it off the ground beside Jim's feet and landing it neatly in front of the jaw-snapping lizard-lion.

Jim spun about and sprinted.

KABOOM!

The beast disappeared back into the flames roaring and spitting, and pieces of concrete launched into the air like mortars—

"My bass!" Mike shouted again, impotently—

crash!—

and a chunk of cheap masonry smashed down in the center of the Impala's roof, crashing through the front seats, driving a hole through the floor of the car and kicking out a cloud of dust and sand as it plowed to rest in the ground underneath.

"My car," he groaned.

"We got bigger troubles than that," Eddie said, jerking open the shotgun door of the van as he threw the bandolier over one shoulder. He pointed into the darkness. "Zvuvim. Keep an eye out for the Baal." From a pocket in the door, he pulled out, of all things, a shotgun. Twelve-gauge, sawed-off. Mike swallowed back the urge to throw up again; a lot of working bands carried some protection, but he'd never seen anyone like these guys.

"Keep my eye on the ball?" he snorted. "What ball?"

Eddie chuckled. "All of them."

Jim raced in the direction Eddie pointed, sword up. Beyond and above him, the things that Mike had thought might be remote control airplanes were coming in. But they weren't airplanes.

They were flies.

Flies the size of Dobermans, with clacking, scythe-like front legs and jaws. They were black and dusty-looking, except for huge eyes that glittered like clusters of Christmas tree ornaments, and enormous jagged mandibles that gleamed like steel and clacked together as they flew.

"Cagado," Mike observed.

"Zvuvim," Eddie said, as if that made any kind of sense at all. "They can be killed."

"They can?" Mike asked weakly. "By what? Giant flypaper?"

"Also, they're kind of stupid until the Baal actually gets on the scene. Twitch!" Eddie shouted. "Get Adrian up now, we need daylight, pronto, or we're dead meat!"

"I'm on it!" Twitch called back.

"Dead meat?" Mike gulped. "I thought you said they could be killed."

"They can," Eddie said, "but there's an awful lot of them." He pumped the shotgun, raised it and fired, blasting one of the giant flies out of the air before it could jump on Jim's back. He stepped forward, pumping the weapon again.

Jim slashed with his sword, backing in a constant quick circle as flies swarmed him like a herd of flying black murderous sheep. He looked like he was trying to scratch them with his blade, rather than impale them, and that made sense to Mike—if the big guy got his weapon stuck inside one fly, the others would pile onto him. A fly zoomed in too close, biting for Jim's knee, and the big guy flipped forward, cartwheeling right over the creature as it missed.

"Twitch!" Eddie called, and aimed at one of the Zvuvim.

Boom!

The shotgun blast shredded the giant fly like a piñata, throwing black flesh and steel shards in all directions.

Mike looked over at Twitch, and then shook his head to clear it before looking again. He would have sworn that the drummer was a man, but from this angle, Twitch looked more feminine than he … she … did before. And he clearly had breasts.

She.

"Come on, Adrian," she said, and she leaned over the boxy organist and her hair fell around them both like a veil. "There's no one here but you and me, you handsome devil, and I need you to cast a little spell."

Mike shook his head. He'd lived with some pretty odd things in his life, sure. He'd been a gangbanger and a thief as a kid, he'd seen death and he'd caused it, and he'd lived all his adult life with a ghost who tormented him and drove him to constant drinking. That, he knew, was more strangeness and darkness than most people ever encountered in their entire lives, and it was enough strangeness and darkness to push him to the edge of suicide. But the step from his brother's ghost to the events of this evening— the swords and guns, the grenades, the gender-ambiguous drummer, the giant fire lizard, the silver horse, the flies as big as wolves—was a giant leap, like the NASA guys might have said.

But the flies were headed his direction, and suddenly Mike found that he didn't want to die, not really. Siding with the band seemed like his only shot. Mike raised the pistol and started firing.

"Come on, lad," he heard from Twitch.

KABOOM!

Another grenade went off, its concussion waves staggering Jim but throwing a carpet of flies off his body.

Mike heard a chittering and a buzzing sound behind him, and he spun, still firing. He should have counted his bullets, he thought as he plugged a fly right between its thousand-faceted eyes just as it was about to plunge steel mandibles into Twitch's back. Oh, well.

Adrian sat up. "Twitch?" he asked. He seemed lucid, but the way he looked only at Twitch despite the fury and chaos all around him gave Mike the impression that the organ player was stoned.

Bang! Mike blew away another … Zvuvim?

ROAR!

A loud crash on the far side of Butcher's warned Mike that the big ugly thing inside had probably smashed down the back wall and freed itself. Any moment, it would be in the parking lot and after blood.

KABOOM!

Another grenade exploded, followed by a series of shotgun blasts.

"Ah, Adrian, you big handsome lunk. I've got you alone at last, and isn't it sweet and quiet here in the meadow?"

Mike would have scratched his head in puzzlement, only he was too busy shooting giant flies. He blew away a second, and then a third, and then—

click.

"Fundillo!"

He jammed the empty gun into his pocket, resisting the urge to throw it away. The open side door of the Dodge van caught his eye, and he lurched over to look inside.

"I do like a picnic," Adrian said. He didn't sound dazed or crazy, but his words were totally nuts. Or stoned. "Where's everybody else?"

The inside of the van was a mess, clothes and crumpled food cartons and maps and coffee cups, and in the back he saw the head of a bass guitar poking up behind the seat. And there were weapons.

Lots of weapons.

Mike grabbed the nearest thing, which was a long-barreled silver revolver, like you'd see in a Clint Eastwood film, Mike thought. He spun the cylinder once to be sure it was loaded, then turned—

and a fly crashed into his chest.

He fell backward, slamming into the side of the van and tumbling to the ground. He couldn't aim, but he fired—

Bang! Bang!

The giant fly stank like sulfur and its flesh was dry and gnarled. Cold steel cut into Mike's shoulder as it bit him.

"Aaagh!" he screamed, and tried to bring the pistol to bear on the thing. The gun's barrel was too long, and he couldn't get it properly aimed at the fly, but he managed to jam one elbow up under the bug's mandibles and hurl it away a couple of feet.

It swarmed back at him and he kicked it with both feet, like a mule, knocking it further away.

It rushed a third time and Mike rolled under the van.

"You'll see everyone else," he heard Twitch tell Adrian. "They're all here. Only it's dark, isn't it? Why don't you cast a little spell, nothing hard, just a little light for us to see by, so we can continue our picnic?"

The fly hit the gravel where Mike had been. It bounced off and for a moment he hoped it would go away, but almost immediately it landed … stayed down … turned … and looked at him. He gulped, trying to scuttle backward on his belly without dropping the pistol.

"I can summon daylight," Adrian said. "I'm good at that," he frowned, "so long as nothing interferes."

The giant fly skittered forward. Beyond the fly, behind Twitch, Mike could see something approaching. It looked like it had feet, might even be a man, but if it was a man then he was covered in swarming flies, like bees around a hive.

"And what could possibly interfere?" Twitch asked.

The fly sprang for Mike's head—

bang!

He shredded it, spattering the underside of the van with its withered, husk-like bits. An explosion of bitter black dust, like gunpowder, made Mike's eyes sting and water. He coughed and slapped at his face, trying to clear his eyes, but he kept moving.

Mike rolled out from under the van. He had a bullet or two left, he was sure, and he raised the revolver, blinking away tears as he stumbled toward the fly-covered man.

Only it wasn't a man. It was man-shaped, but at least eight feet tall. It stank of rotten meat, and when the curtain of flies parted Mike could see that its flesh was the dusty black of a beetle carapace, mottled with gray. Its head was three times too large for its body, with fly-like eyes and tusks like an elephant.

It stepped toward Twitch and Adrian. Mike didn't hesitate.

Bang! Bang! Click.

With each shot, the cloud of flies shifted and the monstrosity stepped back slightly, but it didn't fall, and it didn't bleed.

And then it turned to look at Mike.

"Mierda."

"Per Isidem lux!" Adrian called. He sounded cheerful, like he really was at a picnic, and he waved his hands, in one of which he held a bit of glass.

The parking lot was suddenly full of light. It didn't come from anywhere, it just *was*. And it was the warm and yellow light of day, which was really damn weird, since the sky above still glittered with diamond-like stars in a field of midnight black, but Mike's shadow underneath him looked like the shadow he'd cast at high noon. The high sandstone butte above Butcher's that had been a dark shadow before was now a wall of brilliant red.

Raaaaraaaraarrrghhhhh! shrieked the fly-covered giant.

"Isn't that nice?" Twitch said to Adrian, and pulled his head to her shoulder.

The fly-giant staggered back, swiping at the flesh of its own arms and chest with big, razor-sharp talons. Mike rubbed his eyes to make sure he wasn't seeing things—the swarm of little flies on the big guy's body looked like they were *melting off*. He—it—whatever, lurched away, trying to find the darkness again.

Mike stumbled around the van to the open door and looked for something else to shoot with, or more bullets for the semi-automatic or the revolver. He was interrupted by Jim and Eddie running up behind him.

"I'm almost done here," Twitch said, and she sounded drained and weak.

"Load in," Eddie said. The guitarist grabbed Adrian by one shoulder and yanked him to his feet. Mike noticed that Eddie seemed to have a drifting eye, or some kind of nervous fidget. One of his eyes, anyway, seemed to slide sideways as he manhandled Adrian, and then the guitar player shuddered.

"Hey!" Adrian objected. "Twitch and I were having a conversation. A *private* and *personal* conversation."

"Idiot." Eddie threw the organist onto the back seat of the van. "Hold on, Twitch," he said.

Mike looked around the gravel lot. Butcher's burned in a yellow bubble of light. Just beyond that bubble, Mike could now see that the darkness fell, and in that darkness swarmed flies. "Jeez," he said.

Jim leaped into the driver's seat of the van, shoving his rapier in beside the seat.

"Good luck," Eddie said, and grabbed Mike's hand to shake it. "I'd give you your share of the night's take, but I don't have it. By now, it's probably burnt to a crisp. I suggest you hide."

"My car," Mike said stupidly. If they left him, he'd be sober and alone and without a loaded gun. He found that he didn't want to die, but he *really* didn't want to die nibbled to pieces by gigantic flies.

Twitch staggered over to the van and threw herself in, flopping onto the middle seat and swaying back and forth.

"Where we're going, it only gets worse," Eddie said. He said it gently, like he was breaking a hard truth to a kid, but it was still a no, and it still meant Eddie was going to leave him alone in the desert. "Keep your head down here, you might just make it."

"I need a ride," Mike said. "I can't be out here alone."

Jim pivoted in the driver's seat and stared at Mike. His eyes, Mike now saw, were the color of ice, so blue they were almost white. He stared at Mike intensely for several long seconds, and Mike felt that that big Viking was learning something intensely private about him. He felt naked.

ROAR!

Jim nodded to Eddie, held up a hand palm-first and fingers splayed apart, then started the van.

"Get in!" Eddie said, his tone one hundred percent changed, and shoved Mike with his shoulder to help make it happen. The man was all skin and bone, but he had a gift for leverage, and Mike found himself sitting in the van and the door sliding shut before he could say anything else.

And beyond the door, blazing with blue and black fire and jetting tendrils of smoke from its cracked, dry skin, the lizard-lion beast turned the corner of the smoldering ruins, saw the van and charged.

Eddie jumped into the shotgun seat and slammed the door. "Hellhound at three o'clock," he said to Jim, and started cranking down the window to bring his shotgun to bear.

"Hellhound?" Mike asked.

Jim punched the Dodge into gear and slammed on the gas. The van lurched left onto the two-lane highway and accelerated toward the edge of the bubble of daylight. The flies swarming in the darkness massed around and in front of the van, *chittering* and *clattering* at the edge of the light and waiting for their prey.

"Gone," Twitch muttered, and she slumped against the window.

"Son of a bitch!" Adrian yelled. He sat bolt upright, staring at the Hellhound charging across the gravel.

"Keep it together!" Eddie shouted, and leaned out the window to fire his shotgun. *Boom!* One fly exploded, and its neighbors scattered, but the hole in the wall of demonic fly-flesh immediately sealed shut again. The fly-shrouded giant lumbered with long steps toward the asphalt. "Can you move the light?"

"Of course I can," Adrian said. "If nothing interferes." He patted his pockets and muttered.

The Hellhound was getting closer. Mike scrabbled around in the junk inside the van for a weapon and came up with a big curved Arabian Nights-style sword.

"Good!" Eddie shouted at him with an encouraging grin. "Open the door, and when it gets close, let the thing have it right in the eye!" He turned back to shooting at flies. He looked totally calm and relaxed, which contrasted sharply with Mike's own feeling that the world had turned completely upside down.

Mike yanked on the door handle and pulled it back until it caught. The ground whipped past underneath him unnervingly fast. He wrapped one fist in his seatbelt, watching the Hellhound bound closer over gravel and then over sagebrush, while ahead the tusked giant moved to intercept the van on the highway—

thump!—

the van hit something, maybe a big rock, at the edge of the road, and careened off its wheels at an angle—

Mike slid halfway out the door, only catching himself by the hand he'd tangled up—

the Dodge sailed briefly through the air, and—

thud! crashed to the asphalt again. Twitch slid down the middle seat toward the open door and Mike moved to save her, jamming his body in the way. The leather queen bumped up against Mike's hip before she could recover herself enough to grab onto the seat. She smiled at Mike.

She kind of smiled like a man, Mike thought.

"Hey!" Adrian yelled, clinging with both arms to the seat in front of him. "You can't do that to a wizard! Stay on the road, Jim!"

Eddie blasted another fly and shrugged. "What do you expect from a guy born in the sixteenth century?" he laughed.

Adrian's eyes bugged out like he was about to yell something back—

and instead, he passed out.

Like a snuffed candle, the daylight disappeared.

The van raced pell-mell into the seething cloud of flies, the Hellhound snapping at its rear tires.

CHAPTER THREE

he Zvuvim hit the front of the Dodge van like a black
hailstorm, cracking glass and ripping away the side view
mirrors and the antenna. Only the forward motion of the van
itself, and big, awkward swipes of Mike's borrowed sword, kept
them from swarming in through the open door. Severed antennae
and mandibles and a bit of wing fell into the carpet of detritus
covering the floor of the band's vehicle.

For a split second, Mike hoped the fly-storm would stop the
Hellhound, but he hoped in vain. The Hound roared again, shook
itself to clear off the first swarm of Zvuvim, and then the devil-flies
learned it was there and got out of its way.

Boom!

Eddie leaned back almost into the driver's seat, blowing a fly to
smithereens in his own window. Two more jammed in behind it,
steel mandibles clacketing and grabbing for flesh, and Eddie
jammed a foot against them, kicking at them over and over again
and forcing them out the window while he scrabbled in his pockets
for more shells. Mike noticed Eddie's combat boots, worn and
steel-plated in the toes, and the bandolier on his shoulder, still
holding a single lonely grenade. The flies looked like they might get
Eddie, when suddenly a silver blade flashed into the seething wall
of black—

not from Eddie, but from Jim.

The singer's driving, rough already, didn't suffer much as he wove a net of sharp steel around Eddie's feet. He punctured fly bodies and sliced off wings, keeping his guitarist from being snatched out the window. Mike thought he kept his eyes on the road, coming to Eddie's rescue without even looking, much less breaking a sweat.

Then Mike had to look away to focus on the Hellhound.

The beast lunged for the van's open door, crocodile jaws gaping wide. This close, it struck Mike as looking like a dinosaur: teeth like daggers, hind legs a little bigger than the forelegs, tail thicker than a lion's would really be, eyes glossy black. Only it looked like a dinosaur on fire in three colors.

He yanked himself back into the van with his left hand and avoided a swooping bite of those deadly jaws. Cardboard and vinyl and fast food papers erupted in a small cloud around the Hellhound's bite, the oily paper bags and napkins bursting into flame on contact.

The unblinking eyes, big as saucers, were in reach, and Mike swung for them. His heavy saber hit the Hellhound in the face, sending up sparks as if he'd chipped the blade against a ridge of flint, but he missed the eyes. The thing had a head like a horse, or a tyrannosaurus, a bony ridge with eyes fixed on either side of it, and Mike's saber clanged into the beast's ridge. His blow left no mark.

Still, the creature didn't like it.

The Hellhound thundered in rage. It fell back a step as it did, and inside its gaping maw Mike saw nothing but row after row of knife-long teeth, like a shark's mouth, and sulfurous tendrils of smoke. Not even a tongue.

Boom!

"Brace yourselves!" Eddie shouted.

Mike looked over his shoulder in time to see the man-shaped giant hurl itself against the front of the van.

Crash!

Tusks slammed against the front window in the middle of an enormous face that was part fly and part boar. The van swerved, but Jim grappled the wheel as fiercely as any professional wrestler and kept it on the road. Yellowed talons groped at the edges of Eddie's window and he kicked at them, drawing an irritated squeal from the fly-pig-giant. Still without even looking, Jim reached past Eddie and scratched at the giant's knuckles with his blade. The grenade bounced more wildly on the bandolier on Eddie's shoulder as the van swerved, and Mike worried it might fall off and explode inside the vehicle.

The Hellhound lunged again, jaws wide—

and Mike stabbed, not for the eyes this time, but for the open mouth—

And he jammed his scimitar down deep into the fumes and the bristling spikes, feeling it strike solid flesh and penetrate. Fire and smoke erupted from the wound, scorching his hand and forcing Mike to let go of the sword.

The Hound bellowed in frustration and slowed, shaking its head and pawing at the saber.

"Good one, Mikey," Twitch said. He … she … whatever, seemed recovered. He had his thick drumsticks out again and was clambering around Mike, swinging with them to try to help Eddie and Jim with the big gray thing that still dragged along with the van, trying to force its way into the window.

Boom!

Eddie's shot struck the creature squarely in its fly-like eye, but it only flinched and bellowed, sounding more irritated than hurt. Jim stabbed between its tusks, and some kind of black liquid— aswarm with little flies—sprayed over Eddie and the shotgun seat, but the giant didn't give in or go away.

Twitch lurched over the back of the seat, half-climbing on Mike to swing and batter the creature further in its face with his club. It bellowed again, and grabbed for Twitch, but Jim stabbed it in the arm. The drummer pulled quickly out of reach and Eddie kicked it again. Flies—small, normal-sized flies—filled the air around Eddie and tinted Mike's hearing with an incessant buzz.

"What is that thing?" Mike asked. The Hellhound had somehow yanked the sword from its mouth and was circling around to attack again, so he scrabbled around in the slow waterfall of rubbish trailing out the van's open door for another weapon, without success.

"It's a Baal!" Twitch shouted.

Boom!

The humanoid thing squealed and chittered.

"Ball?" Mike asked. He didn't get it. "As in, *keep my eye on the ball?*"

"Baal, as in Baal Zavuv," Twitch explained, without explaining anything. He leaned forward to crack the Baal another time in the face, and Mike was sure he felt breasts press against his shoulder. With Twitch's blow, the rotten meat stink of the Baal got worse, like she had ripped the skin of a decaying corpse to uncover the corruption beneath.

"Do you mean Zvuvim?"

"One Zavuv—"

Twitch pounded a fly-demon away from Eddie's hip with her baton—

"Two Zvuvim!"

She crunched another between the eyes, its carcass falling into the rubbish on the floor.

"Oh." Mike kicked the dead fly out of the van. He wished it were bigger, so its corpse might actually slow the Hellhound down.

Twitch smacked the Baal again, and the firm decisiveness of her attack, and the resulting pleasant jiggles, made Mike very conscious of her femininity. "And their master is a Baal Zavuv."

The Baal swiped at Twitch, and Jim stabbed its wrist with his sword, the blade darting in like a cobra to sting and pull back.

Graaaaraaaaaaaagh! the Baal objected to being stabbed, and Eddie kicked it in the face. Still it hung on, and the van lurched back and forth as it barreled down the highway.

"Baal ... you mean *Beelzebub?*"

"Now he gets it," Eddie muttered. Only the speed of the van kept the Baal outside, by forcing it to use its hands mostly to hang on. Still, its tusks snapped at Eddie through the cloud of flies, and Eddie kicked for the center of its face and pumped the twelve-gauge again.

"*The* Beelzebub?" Mike felt sick. He grabbed what looked like a gun, but turned out to be a blow dryer. He looked up to see Jim's blade reaching behind Eddie's seatback and skewering a Zavuv, pinning it to the wall of the van. The singer snapped his wrist and tossed the fly-demon off his blade and out the door.

"You're not listening," Twitch said. "It's *a* Baal Zavuv."

"You mean there are others?"

"Oh, lots." Twitch grinned.

Mike looked back out the open door and saw the Hellhound, racing closer and opening its enormous smoking jaw. Desperately, he grabbed for the only weapon he could think of—

Snatching the last grenade off Eddie's bandolier—

With a faint *snick,* the pin decided to stay behind—

And hurling it into the Hellhound's razor-pit maw.

"Duck!" Twitch yelled, and dropped into the pile of junk.

Mike grabbed for the door handle and slammed the door forward, as the Hellhound yakked and fussed at the thing in its jaws, like a cat with a hairball.

KABOOM!

Somehow, maybe because it was inside the Hellhound's mouth, the explosion was bigger than the others had been. The van rocked with the impact, tilting up onto its driver's side wheels, and every window on the passenger side of the vehicle cracked. Fire washed up against the Dodge like a tide.

The Baal, caught by surprise in the moment of trying to slap at Eddie with one of its fists, lost its grip. The explosion threw it up and over the van as the van tilted, jerked it free and hurled it into the sagebrush and shadow on the other side. The headlights just caught a flash of it, gray-black and swarming with flies, tumbling down the side of the road, and then the van's passenger-side wheels touched down with a heavy *thump* and the van burst out of the cloud of Zvuvim and into clear night air.

Mike bounced against the back of the shotgun seat and then collapsed. He was sweating and cold, his heart pounded like a jackhammer in his chest, but the stink of the Baal was gone and cold clean air rushed into the van and he felt like he could breathe for the first time in hours. He looked back and saw jets of multicolored flame inside a dark knot of tangled, twisting air that marked where the evening's strange attackers were.

Twitch got back into her seat and Eddie swiveled again into a normal sitting position, winding his shoulder like he was stretching for a pitch.

"Jeez," Mike said. "Who *are* you guys?"

"Like I told you this morning," Eddie chuckled. "We're a rock band."

"On the phone this morning you forgot to mention the Hellhound."

Eddie shrugged. "We're a rock band that fights evil."

Fights evil? "What, like knights of the round table?"

In the dim light inside the van, Mike saw Eddie's bad eye drift sideways again, and Eddie hesitated before answering. "Not like knights," he said. "More like rival gangsters. We're out to get Satan."

"Before he gets us." Twitch laughed.

"Carajo."

"We're your family now," Twitch added. "Jim took you in."

"You've got the Hand on you," Eddie explained.

Mike met Jim's eyes in the rearview mirror. They were shockingly pale, even in the darkness. "The hand?" Mike asked.

"The Left Hand," Twitch said. "It's a bad thing that Jim agreed to let you in."

"No it isn't," Eddie snorted, and began thumbing shells into the shotgun. "The bad thing would have been getting left behind and eaten."

"And going to Hell, poor boy," Twitch continued.

"I'm going to Hell?" Of course Mike knew he was going to Hell. How did Twitch know it?

"No," Eddie finished, "Jim taking you in is not a bad thing. Look, it's like … it's like getting admitted to the hospital for cancer surgery. It's bad that you have cancer, and getting operated on is no fun, but getting admitted to the hospital is a *good* thing."

"Unless you get an infection," Twitch pointed out.

Mike looked around at the rumpled and torn interior of the Dodge and laughed. He felt shaky. "I haven't been in too many hospitals, but none of them looked like this."

"No," Twitch agreed, "I have it on good authority that this is a nineteen seventy-something Dodge something-or-other."

"You want to get anywhere in this world," Eddie said, "you need a good car."

"You saying this is a good car?"

"Nope." Eddie guffawed. "This is a nineteen seventy-something Dodge something-or-other, and a total piece of crap."

"You got anything to drink in this piece of crap?" Mike asked. He rummaged through the junk at his feet. "Other than cold coffee?"

"You got something against cold coffee," Eddie said, "and we might not be able to be friends."

A sign flared on the side of the road in the Dodge's headlights. Jim swerved toward the sign as if to read it better and nearly ran it over before correcting course and getting the van back into the center of the asphalt, over the dashed yellow line.

DUDAEL, N.M., the sign read.

There was no population indicated.

Twitch handed Mike a small bottle. He smelled spirits, and took a sip without investigating further. He tasted cheap whisky, suffered the burn in his throat and stomach and instantly felt much better. "What's the Left Hand, then?" he asked. He met Jim's eyes again in the mirror. "What did you see, Jim?"

"Jim won't talk," Twitch said. "Don't take it personal."

"It ain't you," Eddie tried to soften the blow. "It's because of Isaiah six."

Mike took another sip, trying to puzzle out the reference. He thought of Eddie's combat boots and grenades. "Is that a military thing?" he asked. "Like a code? Are you guys special forces?"

"No, it's in the Bible." Eddie arched an eyebrow at him. "You know what the Bible is, don't you?"

"Yeah," Mike agreed, "but go easy, I haven't actually read it, I was raised Catholic and we had a priest to do the reading for us. But I know ..." he took a swig and considered, "I know it's got two halves. And Moses and the Israelites are in one half, and Jesus and the saints are in the other."

"This is the Moses half," Eddie said. Mike offered him the bottle, but Eddie shook his head.

"What does Moses say about Jim not talking, then?"

"'In a the year that king Uzziah died,'" Eddie said in a voice that sounded a little bit like a chant, "'I saw also the Lord sitting upon a throne, high and lifted up, and his train filled the temple. Above it stood the seraphim: each one had six wings; with twain he covered his face, and with twain he covered his feet, and with twain he did fly. And one cried unto another, and said, holy, holy, holy, is the Lord of hosts: the whole earth is full of his glory.'"

"Heavy." Mike took a sip, glad he didn't have to drive. "I didn't hear Jim mentioned, though."

"No, Isaiah's talking about the angels in Heaven," Eddie agreed.

"Jim's not an angel."

Mike caught Jim's eye in the rearview mirror and the singer winked.

Eddie and Twitch looked at each other. "No," Eddie agreed, "Jim's not an angel. Here's the thing. The angels in Heaven, what do they do?"

"Holy, holy, holy," Mike said cheerfully. A few more sips of whisky, he thought, and he'd forget the Baal Zavuv, forget the Hellhound, and even, for a little while, forget Chuy. Maybe he'd even forget that he'd wanted to kill himself.

"That's right," Eddie agreed, "they *sing*. They sing in the New Testament … in the *Jesus half*, too. Luke two, 'and suddenly there was with the angel a multitude of the heavenly host praising God, and saying, glory to God in the highest, and on earth peace, good will toward men. And Job says the morning stars sang together, and the sons of God shouted for joy.'"

"Fine," Mike agreed. He didn't care about any of this stuff. "Angels sing."

"So when angels get cast out of Heaven," Eddie continued, as if he was trying to coax Mike to an obvious conclusion, "what do they do?"

Mike scratched his head. "They rap?"

"They don't sing anymore," Twitch explained.

"They can't even *hear* singing," Eddie added. "They can't hear *any* music. Music is Heaven's gift to the angels, and when they rebel, they lose it entirely."

Mike didn't think he'd had enough whisky to make him stupid, but he still couldn't put his finger on the thread. "Jim's not an angel," he repeated.

"Jim won't speak, because he's worried about being heard by the angels. The fallen angels." Eddie nodded encouragingly at Mike, like this all made sense. "But he can sing all he wants."

"But you guys all talk."

"Oh, the Fallen aren't listening for *us,*"Twitch said reassuringly. "Or for *you,* Mikey. You can talk all you want."

This wasn't a hospital, Mike thought. It was an insane asylum. "Don't call me Mikey," he said, a little sullen.

Eddie nodded. "Almost there," he said. "Better get loaded up." He knocked the glove compartment open with his knee and produced a box of forty-five caliber shells, which he passed back to Mike. "Come with us to stick it to Satan. Or stay here and get stuck. Still have the bouncer's pistol?" he asked.

For an answer, Mike produced the pistol and started loading both clips.

"What happened?" Adrian sat upright in the back seat of the van, shaking his head.

"You fell asleep again," Eddie grumped.

"Ah, but first you and I saved the day, big boy," Twitch elaborated, smiling in a beguilingly feminine way. Mike sipped the last of the whisky, dropped the bottle into the rubbish heaped around his own ankles, and tried to think of an inoffensive way to confirm that Twitch was a woman.

"Remind me, next time I need a wizard," Eddie complained to Jim, "to pick one who ain't narcoleptic."

"I'm not narcoleptic," Adrian said, straightening his tie.

"Oh yeah?" Eddie was unconvinced.

"I'm cursed."

"With what?" Eddie asked.

Adrian looked down at the singed knees of his suit. "Narcolepsy," he muttered. "But only in moments of great stress."

"Right," Eddie agreed. "Only when it counts."

"Why are you cursed?" Mike asked. He tried to keep images out of his mind: of Chuy in the basement of the burnt-out school, Chuy getting high on the weed Mike had scored, Chuy and the girl, Chuy cut to ribbons and bleeding to death.

Chuy in Butcher's, taunting him.

"I stole something," Adrian muttered. "I'm not proud of it, but it was the quickest way to get where I needed to go. Faint heart never won, et cetera."

"Or in other words," Eddie summarized, "you're a thief, as well as a narcoleptic."

"As well as a wizard," Adrian said. "Besides, if I was the kind of guy who followed all the rules, I wouldn't really fit in on this team, would I?"

"Touché," Twitch admitted the point. Mike thought Jim's eyes in the rearview mirror looked like they were smiling.

"We're here," Eddie said, and Jim pulled over. The van was still going five or ten miles an hour when he threw it into Park. Mike nearly fell over as the Dodge ground to a squealing, protested halt.

Mike would have been reluctant to get out of the van, but with Twitch and his (her?) batons pushing him from one direction and Adrian shoving from the other, he had no choice. He yanked open the van's side door and went out gun first, looking for the Baal Zavuv, the Zvuvim, or the Hellhound.

He landed a bit wobbly on hard-packed dirt and heard … crickets. Overhead, a lid of a million brilliant stars fell screaming to the horizon, where it clanged off the staunch silhouetted shoulders of the hills and buttes of New Mexico. Other than the starlight, and the light from the Dodge's headlights, the night was pitch black.

"Where's the town?" he asked. "Is this all there is?"

The headlights glared yellow on a building. It was a simple brick-shaped rectangle, two or three stories in height, with some kind of a dome on top. The light reflected on many colors in the glass of the high windows. Some of the windows, anyway; as Mike looked, he could see that a lot of the glass had been smashed out. The woodwork around the windows' frames looked chewed to splinters, and the double-wide door to the building was gone.

Not open … gone.

"I guess now we know why the Hound showed up before the Baal," Eddie said slowly. "The Baal came here first, ahead of us."

"The question is why the Baal and the Hellhound got here at all," Twitch noted. "I thought we traveled under the famous wards of obfuscation."

"So did I," Eddie agreed.

"You can complain about my work," Adrian said bitterly, dropping out of the van onto both feet, "when you can do better. He who is without sin, and so forth." He held a green metal three-gallon gas can in one hand, and it sloshed when he moved.

"Are we too late?" Eddie asked Jim, who stalked around the front of the van with his naked sword in his hand.

Jim shrugged and went into the building. Eddie followed him, and Twitch.

BETH RAZ NIHYEH, read a bronze plaque beside the front door, over a single row of characters that Mike guessed were Hebrew; he'd seen them before, anyway, on Bar Mitzvah programs.

"What kind of place is this?" he asked.

"A synagogue," Adrian said.

Mike pointed at the gas can. "You always carry gasoline into synagogues?"

"This is Dudael," Adrian told him, as if that were an answer. He set the can down, spat into the palms of his own hands to slick back his hair, and then picked up the can again. "Where God ordered the archangel Raphael to imprison Azazel and all the other rebel angels."

"Azazel?"

"You know him better as Satan. Lucifer, if you want to be formal about it."

"What?" Mike almost dropped his pistol. "What are we doing here?"

"Jim's looking for something," Adrian said. "Something in the nature of a family heirloom, you could say." He shrugged. "I suppose you can go back, if you want." Then he disappeared into the building, too.

Mike didn't wait; he jogged in close on Adrian's heels, gun gripped firmly in one hand and the fingers of the other wrapped in the tangle of trinkets on his chest.

The last thing he wanted right now was to be alone in the darkness with Chuy.

CHAPTER FOUR

ait!" Mike called, stumbling through the door. "What's the Left Hand?"

He found himself in a little antechamber, like a cloakroom or a small lobby, and Adrian had already passed through and gone ahead. Mike stopped to look around and let his eyes adjust—light came in from other chambers, but this entry hall was unlit. Mike had been in more than one synagogue, and here he expected to see, once his eyes grew used to the dimmer light, some kind of social space. Like a board, with community notices, maybe, or items relating to the congregation's history, or ads for used cars.

Instead, the room was stark and bare. Off to his right, the chewed-to-bits remnants of a curtain hung over a dimly lit stairway climbing up. Ahead of him was another doorway containing double doors, one of which hung askew on a single hinge while the other lay flat on the floor. Both doors were heavy hardwood affairs, carved with spiral patterns of square Hebrew letters, the bottom of each had been painted gold. To either side of the doorway stood a single stone pillar, smooth and plain. The pillars ended before the ceiling and had nothing on top of them. In the middle of the lobby sat a square block of stone, waist high, that looked like nothing so much as an altar.

"It'd be nice tonight," Mike grumbled out loud to himself, "if just *one thing* turned out to be *normal.*"

He kicked himself forward through the door and found himself several paces behind Adrian. The narcoleptic wizard stood beside the can on the floor, shaking a cramp out of his fingers.

"What's the Left Hand, though?" Mike asked the organ player.

"Ask Eddie that stuff," Adrian said, picking up the can again and huffing slightly from the effort. "I'm the guy you ask when you need to turn invisible or curse someone with the plague."

"You saying you don't know?"

"I'm saying it's not my job."

"Right," Mike muttered, and then he looked around inside the synagogue proper and momentarily forgot his question.

Most of the building was a single long, tall room. Rows of pews had once run from the doors up to the front of the room, Mike could tell, but only a few of them were still standing. The rest looked like they had been run through a wood chipper, their stuffing and covering fabric resting on top of the shattered and splintered hardwood like a coverlet of snow over a junkyard. A mezzanine story full of similarly destroyed seating ran around the back half of the room, and around the entire second-story wall, evenly spaced, were tall stained glass windows, many of them smashed out completely. Mike couldn't see well, but he could see because a few incandescent bulbs had survived the general devastation and now shed weak yellow light on the wreckage.

Mike limped up the hardwood floor along what had once been a central aisle among the pews. The walls below the mezzanine and under the windows, he now saw, were hung with long curtains like tapestries. It was hard to see very well in this light, and the tapestries looked faded, but the images he could make out woven into their fabric were weird and old. Angels fought with dragons; serpents threatened a throne sitting on top of a cloud; angels were chained and thrown into a pit.

Thud.

Mike heard something and jumped. He looked around, not sure what it had been. The entire band was ahead of him, but the noise had come from his left. He looked and saw nothing moving. Rats in the walls, maybe. He shook off an involuntary shiver and continued looking around.

The ceiling overhead was carved and painted, and the cloudy throne was there, too, surrounded by twelve images that Mike at first assumed were the Zodiac. Then he actually managed to make out a few of the faded, unlit signs and saw a ship … another was a deer … a third was a tree branch, and then Mike shook his head. He didn't believe in the Zodiac any more than he believed in the lottery, but he was pretty sure those signs weren't in it. He wrote it off as one more oddity in an already very odd night, and focused back on where he was going.

At the front of the pews and to one side, a platform, like a pulpit with its own stairs, stood astride two steps that climbed to a low dais in front; the pulpit had been gnawed to a misshapen stump. An iron candlestick lay knocked to the ground before the pulpit, its seven arms carved like flowering branches. Beside it were the two shattered halves of a table.

Beyond the pulpit, there was a human body. He was an old man in a dark blue suit, with gray hair and beard, his feet and shoulder jammed against something that forced his knees and head into the air. He was pinned onto the lid of a big wooden chest with what looked like a wooden stake, pushed all the way through his torso and into the wooden container beneath. Death was always ugly, and Mike had seen his share, but he'd never seen it this ugly, or weird. He couldn't see blood anywhere, despite the gaping hole in the man's body. The chest underneath him had two sphinxes carved into its lid, facing left and right away from each other.

The old guy was still moving, though not very much. He muttered something inaudible, just a gasp through twitching lips—

and his skin bubbled. It crawled, and jumped and wiggled like it was loose over the body it covered, and something small, a thousand small somethings, were crawling all over underneath it.

"Jeez." Mike stopped just inside the gnawed-down pulpit and stared. "Vampire?"

"Worse," Twitch shook her head. "Rabbi."

"Is he alive?" Eddie asked. The five of them stood around the man, several steps back.

Adrian set down the can and whipped a clear glass lens from his suit pocket. He squinted through it at the man in the suit. "No," he said. "But he isn't dead, either."

"Will he talk to us?" Eddie asked. The guitarist held his shotgun at the ready and kept looking around the mezzanine.

"Sure he will," Adrian said. He put away the lens, unscrewed the cap of the gas can and began to back around the man on the chest, pouring a trickle of gasoline on the floor as he went. The petroleum stink snapped Mike out of his reverie.

"How did you lose the last bass player?" he asked. "Speaking of … you know … all the crazy stuff I've seen tonight."

Jim walked away from the circle of conversation. He kicked over large boards in the shattered wreckage of the pews and looked around and behind things and generally searched.

"We didn't lose him, big boy," Twitch said. "We know right where he is."

"He died." Eddie's wandering eye snapped spastically in its socket and he closed both his eyes briefly, taking a deep breath.

Mike gulped and tightened his grip on the pistol. "Drug overdose?" he asked hopefully.

Eddie shook his head. "Impaled on his own bass."

"Stand back or get gas on your shoes," Adrian warned. "I need a perfect circle."

"Or what?" Eddie asked. "You might fall asleep?" Jim put a restraining hand on Eddie's shoulder.

"No pressure, Adrian," Twitch said soothingly.

Mike stepped back and watched Adrian finish his circle, then light it with a matchbook he extracted from his pocket. Flames rose from the circle of gas, and when Adrian waved his hand over them, they rose even higher.

"Anyone know the rabbi's name?" Adrian asked.

"Feldman," Eddie supplied the answer.

"No true name? Not even a first name, that's it, just Feldman?"

Eddie looked at Jim, who was poking around the ruined stump of the pulpit. The singer shrugged and nodded.

"That's it," Eddie said. "No sweat, for a man of your talent."

"Makes you feel better about the tambourine, though, don't it?" Twitch asked Eddie. There was a mischievous glint in the drummer's eye. "The whole incident with the bass, that is. I mean, when was the last time you heard of a tambourine player murdered with his own instrument?"

"A tambourine could be sharpened," Eddie said sourly.

"Murdered?" Mike asked.

"Of course," Eddie snapped. "What kind of idiot would it take to impale *himself* on a bass guitar?"

"If there were such an idiot," Twitch observed, "he'd surely be a member of this band."

"What's the Left Hand?" Mike asked again.

"Don't worry about it," Eddie said. "I'll tell you later."

"It's easy," Twitch said. "At the Judgment, everyone gets sorted. They're either on the Right Hand of God—that's really, really good—or they're on His Left. That's terrible. And people who have the Left Hand on them already in life, why, they're damned. All this, of course, pertaining to humans, and other folk who are judged."

Mike strained to listen to Twitch's voice, trying to fathom his (her?) sex so hard, he almost missed the words Twitch said. "Are you—" he asked, about to guess *a woman*, but then he caught the significance of some of Twitch's words. "Do you mean I'm *damned?*" He knew that he was damned, had known it his entire adult life, but it wasn't anyone else's business and he wondered how Jim could possibly see that. "And do you mean some people *aren't* judged *at all?*" he asked. "What does that mean? And why would Jim want to rescue me just because I'm … because I have the Left Hand on me? What is he, like a priest?"

"Jim has a grudge," Eddie said.

Jim kicked the candlestick, hard; it banged loudly against the floor.

"Against what?" Mike gripped the pistol in his hand, the sheer solidity of the gun an antidote to all the insanity he was seeing and hearing around him. He could feel the weight of his various charms and holy symbols at his sternum, too, but got very little comfort from that. "Against damned people? Against saved people?"

"Against Hell," Twitch said. "Eddie told you. We're sticking it to His Lowness."

"Shut up," Adrian growled. "I don't jabber at you when you're trying to find the groove, do I? Do unto others, well, you know." The short man straightened his tie, and then waved both hands over the circle of flame, fluttering the fingers of one hand while clenching his other in a fist. *"Per Osiridem te invoco, o Feldman, ad nos veni!"*

The twitching increased. Mike thought he could see individual mites under Rabbi Feldman's skin, like rapidly migrating blisters. He arched his back, pushing off the chest with his heels and shoulder blades, and lifting his body on the spike that pinned him.

"What's wrong with him?" Mike whispered to Eddie, who stood closest to him. "Is that a disease?"

"Shush," Eddie said.

"More like an infestation," Twitch whispered back. She picked up the gas can and held it ready, but ready for what, Mike didn't know.

"Careful," he suggested. "We don't want to burn the place down."

"Not yet," Twitch agreed.

"Veni ad nos!" Adrian repeated. He was making the same arm and finger gestures, but they were getting faster and faster and he looked frustrated. *"Tavo lanu, Rabbi Feldman, bashem hakodesh!"*

Feldman's arms twitched and his legs trembled, like a break-dancer with only one move, and not a very good one. The wooden spike kept him pinned, but his mouth opened and shut fiercely now, so hard Mike could hear his teeth *click*.

Adrian wiped sweat off his forehead with his sleeve. Mike did the same, in sympathy, but the cracked brown leather of his jacket smeared the sweat around rather than wiping any of it off.

"Veni!" the wizard shouted. Veins stood out in his temples and in his wrists, like dancing snakes, and his face was bright red. *"Veni per Yahweh Sabaoth! Per Yahweh Sabaoth Luciferemque te jubeo, veni!"*

He stamped his feet and the circle of flames raced skyward with a huge *BOOM!*—

And then Adrian crumpled to the floor, and the flames snuffed out.

"Huevos," Mike said, though he wasn't sure why. The dying of Adrian's magical fires made the room, if anything, slightly more normal.

"Did you hear that?" Twitch asked. She set down the can and started walking across the room, turning her head this way and that as she went. The horse's tail protruding from the seat of her black leather outfit swished as she walked, and Mike couldn't help watching it for a few seconds, until he remembered that he wasn't one hundred percent sure Twitch was a woman.

Mike jerked his gaze away.

Then he remembered the *thud* he had heard earlier.

"You mean the explosion?" he called to her (he hoped). "I think they heard that in *Dallas.*" She ignored him, peering behind pews and turning over stray boards to look underneath them. "Could be rats!"

Jim returned to the group around the rabbi. He and Eddie stood over the body of the Rabbi Feldman, who continued to writhe spastically. Mike joined them. There was a bad smell about the body that he recognized, though he couldn't immediately place it, and its mouth seemed to be full of something black. Like caviar, he thought. Someone had stuffed the rabbi with moving caviar.

That stank of rotting meat.

"What's with Twitch?" Mike asked. "She thinks she heard something."

"Horses have great hearing," Eddie said dismissively. "You're right, she probably heard a rat."

So she was female, then. Mike shot a guilt-free glance at Twitch's tail again. Then he realized what Eddie had said.

"Wait a minute," he tried to rewind the conversation. "Horses?"

The guitarist ignored him and talked to Jim in low, urgent tones. "Are you sure the name isn't just a coincidence?" Eddie asked him. "For all I know, *Dudael* is the Hopi word for *Chlamydia.*" He looked around at the shattered synagogue. "Though Heaven knows it looks the part," he said.

The big singer took the rabbi's right hand in his own and turned it palm-up. The old man had a tattoo on his right wrist, bright and black like he'd gotten it recently, and shaped like a candlestick with seven branches. Jim and Eddie exchanged a look.

"We don't have much time," Eddie said. "If that Baal Zavuv found this place before, it's sure as hell on its way here now."

"Let's just leave," Mike suggested.

"Do something useful," Eddie snapped. "Wake up Adrian, maybe."

Mike had just enough booze in him not to take offense. "What kind of thing are you looking for, Jim?" he asked as he crouched over Adrian's unconscious body and slapped the other man in the face. "Maybe I can help."

"Jim's not going to talk to you," Eddie reminded Mike through gritted teeth. "And we're not looking for a *thing*, we're looking for a *place*."

"Well, did we find it, then?" Mike pressed.

"Over here!" Twitch shouted from halfway across the room. She was poking open the trapdoor of something that looked like an oversized mail slot, built right into the wall. It was about where Mike had heard the noise earlier, he thought.

Jim immediately ran to join her, and Eddie followed at a walk, shotgun at the ready. "What is that, the *genizah?*" he shouted.

"What's a *genizah?*" Mike asked, his head spinning. "And is it more or less dangerous than a Baal Zavuv?"

"It's a cabinet," Eddie said as he broke into a jog, "full of books that are too old to use and too holy to throw away." He called back to Mike over his shoulder, without looking. "Get Adrian up! We need Feldman to show us the way forward!"

Mike went back to the scene of the failed summoning, scratching his head at what to do. Adrian snored gently, so he started by pinching the sorcerer's nose and twisting it sharply clockwise—no effect. He thought of Twitch, and how the drummer had awoken the wizard earlier.

"Come on, big boy," he said awkwardly. "It's just you and me, and everything is hunky-dory." His own words made him feel uncomfortable. He rapped Adrian on the forehead with his knuckle. "Everything is nice and easy, no pressure. Let's have a picnic." Mike cleared his throat and looked around to be sure no one was watching him. The thought that he might see Chuy made him a little nervous, but he guessed that he had enough liquor in him to hold the apparition at bay for the moment. He hoped he did.

The rabbi's twitches were getting more extreme. He flopped around like a live fish on a hot sidewalk, and Mike frowned. What was that black stuff bubbling up between the old man's teeth?

And why had Twitch picked up the gas can earlier? What was it she had said … that the rabbi was *infested?*

Mike stood up and stretched to get a better look at Rabbi Feldman. The substance bubbling inside his mouth was beginning to well up past his lips and spill down onto his throat, and onto the chest on which he lay. It was black as tar, but was formed into discrete globes. Just like caviar, Mike thought, not that he'd eaten much caviar himself, other than what he'd stolen from weddings he'd played at. Only each of the bubbles was quivering, and as they fell and hit the floor, they continued to shake and roll around.

And the rabbi stank of rotting meat.

Just like the Baal Zavuv.

"Guys?" he called it. "This doesn't look very good."

There was no answer. He looked over at Jim, Eddie and Twitch, and saw that they were helping a person—someone really small—a skinny little *kid,* actually, crawl out of a hole they'd smashed in the wall.

He kicked Adrian. "Wake up!" he barked.

Nothing.

How would he light the gas, if he had to? He remembered Adrian's book of matches, pushed the pistol into the back of his belt and got down again to shove his hands into Adrian's pockets until he found it. *GOLDEN DAWN MOTEL,* read the scratched and faded lettering on the little black book, or maybe it was *GOLDEN SANDS*, he couldn't be sure, *AMARILLO*. It smelled like ammonia and the cardboard was fraying, but if the Golden Dawn gave guests matches with their name on it, Mike had stayed in places that were worse.

"Guys?" he called again, and stood up to look at Feldman.

The rabbi's face was covered in a black foam of the jiggling little bubbles. Bubbles were squeezing up around the spike in his chest, too. One of them had bobbled its way down one leg of the rabbi's trousers and quivered beside his ankle, like a tiny little blob of sphinx poop. Mike stooped to look at it.

"Cagado," he muttered.

Inside the bubble, behind a black film that swirled like oil on a puddle, he could clearly see a fly. It was as big as a horsefly and its mandibles glittered like metal.

He kicked Adrian again, really hard this time, and in the stomach.

"Oomph!" Adrian bellowed, and woke up. He curled reflexively, wrapping himself around Mike's foot and tripping him. Mike fell backward—

hit the floor—

and banged the back of his head against the gas can.

"No!" he gasped, scrabbling at the can with both hands—

as it slowly tipped over—

and Mike missed, the can hit the ground and the gas sloshed out. On the hardwood floor it puddled under the sphinx chest and the rabbi's body.

"What are you doing?" Adrian grunted, and clambered to his feet. His eyes widened. "Hey!"

Mike followed Adrian's eyes from where he lay on the floor, and saw that Rabbi Feldman's body was covered in black foam. No, he realized, it wasn't foam anymore. It was a cloud, coalescing and rising off the body.

A cloud of flies.

"Carajo!" Mike yelped. He grabbed the book of matches and fumbled to pull one of them out. The back of his ears felt wet and he wondered if he'd cut his head in the fall. He'd have to check later.

"Per Isidem ..." Adrian intoned, and then staggered back, sucking in oxygen like he'd emerged from long minutes underwater. *"Per Isidem ..."* His eyes rolled back into his head and he struggled not to swoon.

"Help!" Mike shouted, snapped one of the matches into flame—

"Don't!" he heard Eddie yell—

and he tossed the match over his head.

Whoosh!

"Aaagh!" Mike roared in sudden agony and rolled away from the sudden explosion of light and heat behind him. His shoulders and upper back were on fire—literally. He stumbled like a one-legged sprinter past Adrian, who waggled his fingers over his head and tried again to get out a spell.

Water ... he thought. His back and the back of his head burned.

No, a tapestry … he lurched around, trying to find the nearest wall hanging.

The room exploded into whizzing particles of light, and with a sinking feeling in his heart and stomach, Mike realized that he hadn't stopped the flies, he'd only lit them on fire. Now they raced about the room in all directions, shining with flame and trailing smoke that stank of sulfur, rotting meat and gasoline. They flew zigzag like dandelion spores of light, or like Leonids unconstrained by gravity, racing out in all directions from Rabbi Feldman's funeral pyre.

"Hold still!" Mike wasn't sure who was shouting.

But burning insects hit Mike and stung him, on his legs and his back and his arms, and he couldn't stop running. He smelled a terrible stink and realized it was his own hair and flesh burning, and he kicked and stumbled through the rubble of former pews, trying to get to the wall and a tapestry.

Ahead of him he saw the small silver horse again, and the sight rang a bell in his brain that he was too panicked, and in too much pain, to listen to. A little skinny boy in ill-fitting jeans, white t-shirt and unlaced trainers clung to the back of the animal. He held onto its long silver mane as the horse reared, its hooves trampling a heap of large scrolls that spilled out of a hole in the wall.

Beyond the unexpected horse and its mystery rider, Jim stood with his back to Mike, raising his sword, facing the synagogue door—through which swarmed a funnel cloud of Zvuvim.

CHAPTER FIVE

ot you!" Eddie shouted as he tackled Mike.

The guitarist hit him from behind and right on the shoulders and the back of his neck, where he was burning. It hurt and Mike screamed, but Eddie had his jacket in his hands, and as he dragged Mike to the floor he beat at his body, snuffing out flames.

"Aaagh!" Mike screamed again. He pounded his fist on the floor in pain, grateful that at least he wasn't totally sober. He wished he were a hell of a lot more drunk, though.

Then Eddie was up again and shrugging into his jacket. "Incoming!" the guitar player shouted, and brought his twelve-gauge to bear on the swarming cloud of giant flies.

Boom! Boom!

Mike climbed to his feet, feeling fat and fried and chopped to pieces, like a roaster in a chicken rotisserie. The Zvuvim raged in through the front door of the synagogue in a chittering cloud, and the rabbi's burning corpse-flies buzzed forth from the depths of the hall to meet them, a swarm of glittering candle-points that sparkled and winked from within the black mass.

Jim stood in the doorway, heaving the flattened door off the ground with one hand while he slashed at attacking Zvuvim with the sword in his other. He moved like a matador, avoiding flies by throwing every other part of his body out of the way but holding his hand, and the door it pushed up, fixed in place. Eddie charged in his direction, shotgun up and firing, blasting flies out of the air with each squeeze of the trigger. They swarmed so thick now that it was impossible to miss, and the challenge was to hit the one you were aiming at, and not a different Zavuv that got in the way.

Bang!

Mike squeezed the trigger of the pistol, not remembering when he'd pulled it from his belt, and shattered a dive-bombing Zavuv into stringy black fragments.

The silver horse took off at a gallop with the boy on its back, away from the Zvuvim and around the wall of the synagogue.

The kid, Mike thought. It was the kid who had made the noise he'd heard, not rats. Rats would have been less weird, though, than a kid hiding in a … what had Eddie said? A cabinet full of old books no one could read anymore?

"Get over here!" Eddie yelled.

Boom!

Mike blasted another Zavuv and raced to join Jim and Eddie. Jim had shoved the fallen door back into place and Eddie now held it up with his back, shoving shells into the twelve-gauge and ducking fly attacks. Jim squatted to try to muscle the hanging door up as well, but two Zvuvim clinging to the hardwood slashed and bit at his hands. He bled and grunted and swatted at them with the hilt of his sword, but he made no progress with the door.

Bang!

Mike blew one of the Zvuvim to bits and the other jerked away into the air, *chittering*. Jim got his shoulder under it and slammed the door into place.

"We need wards of sealing here," Eddie said, and Jim nodded.

"It's no good," Mike panted, pointing up at the shattered windows of the second story. The windows were narrow, but only narrow enough that they forced the Zvuvim to crawl through, rather than flying at top speed. "They can get in up there." He fired three more shots, exploding two Zvuvim in the air and a third that crawled rasping along the ceiling beneath the floor of the mezzanine.

"You're forgetting the Baal," Eddie said. "And the Hound. Adrian!" he shouted. "Show me some love!"

Adrian stumbled to the door, batting away burning flies with his left hand. In his right, he held the machine pistol that Mike had first seen back in Butcher's roadhouse. "What's Twitch up to?" the wizard grumbled. "We must all hang together, et cetera."

"Twitch is looking for the way *out!*" Eddie barked. "Your job is to cork up the way *in!*" He took aim at a Zavuv winging in low behind Adrian's back and blew it to kingdom come. The shotgun reports sounded louder under the mezzanine, with an instant slapback echo like a guitar running through a pedal set to one hundred milliseconds of delay.

Mike shook the distracting thought out of his head.

ROAR!

The sound came from outside the synagogue, but it was as loud as the crashing of Niagara Falls.

"Will it help if I tell you we're at a picnic?" Mike offered tentatively.

"Piss off!" Adrian snapped, pushing his pistol into a shoulder holster under his scorched suit jacket and digging two pieces of chalk from his pocket. "And get out of the way."

Mike shrugged. He only wanted to help.

Then he and Eddie peeled aside and stood guard—Jim stepped away from the door but kept one hand up against both panels, pinning them in place as Adrian began to draw pictures on the panels with chalk in two colors, blue and red. Mike took potshots at any Zavuv that got too close to him, but the big black flies seemed to be swarming a little mindlessly. The little flies, at least, burned to extinction one by one and dropped to the floor, leaving the room lit by dim bulbs here and there and the funeral pyre of Rabbi Feldman.

The white horse continued its gallop around the perimeter of the synagogue, plunging under the mezzanine and getting closer to them.

"Don't fall asleep!" Eddie snapped, and threw an elbow into Adrian's ribs.

"Unnh, huh? Hell!" Adrian stumbled and hastily wiped away a long red scrawl down the wood that he had made in the moment of nodding off.

Jim began to hum. Mike couldn't think of the name of the tune, but he would have sworn he knew it from somewhere. It was like one of those songs that you learn as a kid in school, and you never hear again, until you're an old man and you hear some other little kid singing it, and you don't know why you know the tune but you know it.

Adrian nodded and resumed drawing. "Okay, yeah," he muttered. "Wards of sealing. That'll hold them shut for a while."

Mike looked over his shoulder to get a better look at the drawing. It was ornate and in two colors and it covered both doors roughly in a design that looked part spider web, part clock interior, all gears and radiating spokes and here and there a character Mike recognized as being Greek or Hebrew, or didn't recognize at all.

Jim stepped away from the doors, and they stayed standing.

"Now listen to me, my son," Mike heard Twitch say in a gentle, extremely feminine voice, "I need you to show mama your hiding place. The secret one. The secret way out that your father showed you."

Mike was surprised to find Twitch at his elbow again, kneeling and cradling the little boy in his arms. And then he realized that he shouldn't have been surprised, that there was a perfectly logical explanation for Twitch's appearances and disappearances … only the logic in question was the logic of madness.

The kid didn't look like he could be named *Feldman*—he looked Chicano, like he could have fit in perfectly with Mike and Chuy and all their cousins when they were kids, even wearing the same cheap clothes that were always a little too big because it was cheaper to buy them that way—a skinny little kid under a mop of thick black hair. He looked calm, even blissful in Twitch's arms, like he really thought she was his mama.

"I don't know my father," the boy said.

"Not your dad," Mike said. "Rabbi Feldman."

The kid looked at Mike, his face suddenly contorting into a mask of terror.

Boom!

"Hurry it up," Eddie grumped, pumping the shotgun to chamber another round.

"Hush, baby," Twitch purred, and Mike thought he saw the tail on her rump swish back and forth. The boy calmed right down. Mike wondered whether the kid was scared of him, or he had just broken the spell of Twitch's voice. Obviously, there was something more than just simple soothing words going on, since Mike had seen it work on the wizard and the little boy both. "I meant the rabbi."

The walls of the synagogue shook and the sealed doors bowed slightly inward as something outside hammered into them, hard. Something really, really big and strong. Grains of chalk shook off the door and drifted down toward the ground.

The little kid didn't seem to notice. "Yes, mama," he said, and he started walking back toward the burning corpse of Rabbi Feldman, pulling Twitch by the hand.

"The wards of sealing will hold, right?" Eddie demanded as they all followed.

"They'll keep the door shut," Adrian said. "They can't stop it from getting pounded into smithereens."

Eddie coughed out a bitter laugh. "Remind me to get a competent wizard next time."

"*You* don't want a *wizard*," Adrian snorted. "*You* want a *Jedi Knight.*"

"Damn straight," Eddie agreed. "Or a Company of United States Marines." He fired several shells at a knot of approaching fly-demons, bursting some and scattering the rest of them in agitated buzzing circles.

"You …" Mike whispered to Twitch as he followed. "You're the horse."

"Well," she smiled softly and whispered back, "I've never had any complaints from the ladies."

Mike's jaw worked of its own accord for a few long moments, opening and shutting his mouth wordlessly.

"I …" he finally said.

"Yes, Mikey," she (he?) answered. "It's a big world, full of crazier stuff than you can ever possibly guess. I think your Shakespeare said that."

"He did?" Mike was too astonished to object to being called *Mikey*, and he didn't know what to make of the Shakespeare reference. He had dropped out of school long before they ever got around to William Shakespeare. "I mean, he isn't *my* Shakespeare. He wasn't one of my people."

"Oh, sure he was," Twitch said. "People guess all kinds of mysterious things about that poor young man, but I knew him … *well* … and I can assure you that he was very definitely *human*."

"And you're a horse," Mike repeated himself, feeling stupid.

"No, silly," she said. "Not all of the time."

The little kid stopped, and Twitch and Mike stopped with him. Adrian cleared Zvuvim off to one side of them with long *rat-tat-tat-tat-tat* sweeps of his machine pistol, and Eddie guarded the other flank with his shotgun. "There it is." The boy pointed at the flaming wreck of the chest, with Rabbi Feldman's charred corpse smoldering over wood that had collapsed into glowing coals.

The doors resounded to the sound of another mighty blow, and Mike looked back over his shoulder, through the cloud of swarming demonic flies. Chalk sifted down from Adrian's designs, but the doors held.

"Poor kid," Mike muttered, turning back to look at the kid pointing earnestly at the toasted rabbi. "He's got a death wish."

"What do you mean, darling?" Twitch asked the boy. "Show me."

"Under," the boy told her. His voice was a little dazed, like he might be in shock. "Under the ark."

"Poor dumb kid," Mike groaned, and couldn't help but think of Chuy. Chuy had only been a kid too, really, a criminal many times over but not yet eighteen, when Mike had led him to his death. He hadn't meant to, but he'd done it. "He thinks we're on a boat."

But as soon as the kid spoke, Jim dropped his sword to the floor. The singer grabbed both halves of the broken table beside the pyre, shoving one into Mike's hands and turning to the fire himself.

"Huh?" Mike fumbled.

"Shovel!" Eddie shouted. *Boom!* "Shovel like your life depended on it!"

"It does," Adrian affirmed. *Rat-tat-tat-tat-tat.*

The Hellhound bellowed again, so loud Mike thought he felt his own spine tremble with the sound. The Zvuvim seemed to be getting smarter, and they swarmed in closer, diving and clacking their steel mandibles together greedily. Eddie and Adrian kept them off with a ceaseless chatter of gunfire.

Jim pressed his half-table to the floor like a squeegee and Mike followed him clumsily, feeling fat and slow next to the lean, broad-shouldered giant of a singer. He grunted with effort and proximity to the hot coals, and Jim snorted air through his nostrils, and they fell forward and the weight of their bodies brushed away the stinking inferno—

and Mike saw the outline of a trap door, made of scorched hardwood, with an iron ring bolted into it.

CRASH!

Mike stumbled to his feet and whirled to see the Baal Zavuv, tall and gray-black as it charged forward through the splintered remains of the synagogue door, its cloak of flies buzzing frenetically to keep up. At the demon's heels came the Hellhound, adding blue and black tints to the weird, patchy light inside the building.

"Adrian!" Eddie shouted. "I need daylight!"

"Oh yeah?" Adrian shouted back, blasting a Zavuv away from Eddie's back and slapping a new clip into his gun. "Shall I just set the gun down, then?" *Rat-tat-tat-tat-tat.* "Between the devil and all that jazz!"

Twitch dropped the little boy's hand and jumped to Adrian's side, flailing with a wooden club in each hand and knocking demon-flies away like so many low-hanging apples in an orchard.

Jim grabbed the iron ring and heaved. A groan escaped his lips and Mike saw smoke curl up from around his fingers. The ring, he realized, had to be hot, and the thought of the pain that Jim must be feeling made Mike's back and shoulders and the back of his head ache. He dreaded looking in a mirror.

"Mike!" Eddie yelled, and he realized he was standing in the middle of the action and doing nothing. He drew a bead on the Zvuvim over Adrian's head and started shooting.

In the meantime, Jim had lifted the trapdoor to a vertical position. Stone steps, rough-hewn and worn down really deep in the center of each step, descended into darkness. Jim grabbed the little kid and tossed him down the stairs over a short yelp of objection.

The Hellhound bellowed behind Mike, and with the bellow came a slobbery chittering squeal that he recognized as the Baal's. He spun and fired without aiming, *bang! bang! bang!*

He thought he could smell the Baal's meat-stink from across the synagogue.

"Per Isidem lux!" Adrian shouted, and light exploded from behind Mike and flashed onto the charging Baal Zavuv and Hellhound. It was a palpable wave, like a flashbulb's glare, and when it hit the Baal, the great gray demon lord shrieked in pain and crashed to the ground, flailing and dragging the Hound with it. Zvuvim fell from the sky like volcanic ash, stunned and writhing in surprise.

But the light died in a single flash and Mike knew that the soft *thump* he heard immediately after was the sound of Adrian's body hitting the floor.

"Down the hole!" Eddie shouted. Mike fired off the rest of his clip for good measure, spraying fire all over the tangled knot of demon-flesh without inflicting any damage he could see, then stuck the gun in his belt, grabbed one of Adrian's arms and, with Twitch pulling on the other side, dragged the unconscious wizard through the trapdoor.

The first descent was insane, a sightless stumbling down steps that were irregular in every dimension, and several times Mike stubbed his toes or smacked his head or skinned his knuckles against the walls and ceiling of the passage, or landed bad enough that he thought he had twisted an ankle.

When he was halfway down, the trapdoor above slammed shut with a *clang!* and Mike plunged into womb-blind darkness.

Then he hit a smooth patch, a leveling out of the passage, and he and Twitch and Adrian fell together in a heap.

"Are you alright, son?" he heard Twitch say in the dark. He thought she smelled a little horsey, this close.

Adrian groaned, lying under Mike.

"You can see?" Mike asked.

Then a light snapped on above Mike, and after he blinked away the sting of it he realized it was a flashlight beam. The beam jogged down the stairs to Mike's level as he stood up, and then a second beam snapped on near the first, and Eddie materialized in the white beams of illumination, pressing a crosshatch-gripped Maglite into Mike's hands.

"I don't know how far we have to go," Eddie muttered, "but I know that dawn ain't nowhere near close enough to save us."

"What is that, just a bit of random encouragement?" Mike touched the back of his neck—the skin there felt crisp like cooked pastry dough, and stung fiercely at the contact of his fingers. "Just want to make sure my hopes are set at the right level?"

"Exactly," Eddie agreed. "I've got the back, Jim will carry Adrian and Twitch can lead the boy."

"The boy?" Mike swiveled around with his flashlight and found the kid, staring with big brown eyes at the rock band of freaks and lunatics from out of town that had burned down his synagogue.

"We're not leaving the boy," Eddie explained. "Jim wouldn't have it."

"The boy's got the Left Hand on him?" Mike gulped, wondering what the kid could have done to be in such bad spiritual shape.

But Jim shook his head *no* before he turned and bent over to pick Adrian up and sling the organist over his shoulders. Now that the reek of Rabbi Feldman's pyre and the stench of the Baal Zavuv were gone, Mike could smell the scorched flesh of Jim's hands. Or his own back and neck, he realized.

"Nah," Eddie chewed out the words while stretching his shoulders and neck. "Jim just likes pissing off anything and anyone associated with the Infernal powers."

"You mean Hell?"

"I mean Hell," Eddie agreed. "You take point."

The sound of something thudding against the trapdoor echoed down the stairs and kicked Mike into action, sending him shuffling ahead of Jim and Twitch and into the lead. The ceiling of the passageway was mostly over his head, so he gripped the Maglite in his teeth and thumbed shells into the pistol's clips as he walked. The sound of loud clicks behind him suggested that Eddie might be performing a similar action with his twelve-gauge. Mike felt better when the pistol had a fully loaded clip in it.

He would have felt even better with more alcohol in him. He was starting to feel distressingly sober.

The passage looked like it was a natural cave, to Mike's inexpert eye, but the walls of both sides were honeycombed with large holes of some sort. The puffing of his own breath around the flashlight obscured his vision a bit, as each step he took was into a fog of his own making. His footsteps were loud and crunchy in the darkness. He walked fast, conscious of the demonic things somewhere at his back, and shoved bullets into his second clip as fast as he could manage.

When both clips were loaded and the gun back on his belt he realized he didn't hear the footsteps of the others behind him. He stopped, and then his curiosity finally got the better of him. He took the light in his hand, and poked his head into one of the holes. The depression in the wall was barrel-sized and sank down away from the passage. He shone the light down and looked to see what was inside.

The depression was full of skulls.

A hand from the darkness grabbed his wrist.

"Chingado!" Mike shouted.

"No seas maricón!" Chuy hissed, spattering blood from his lips. "You gonna call your friends, you chickenshit *joto?* You think you can make me do anything I don't wanna do anymore?"

"Jeez," Mike panted, trying not to look at his brother's ghost. Chuy stood in shadow, but Mike thought he could see every cut and every drop of blood on the mutilated specter. "Jeez, Chuy ..."

"You don't get away from me, *hijo de puta, comprendes?* You're blood, and that means you're mine forever, you got it?" Chuy's teeth shone white as the moon behind the sheets and rivulets of blood that fell from them and spilled out his mouth. He looked like a wild beast, feeding. "I'm gonna teach *you* a lesson, this time!"

Mike wanted to pull back but the hand held him. Chuy's face danced in rage.

"Chuy, I ... I never ..."

"You never what, *puto que eres? Me cago en ti!"*

A loud boom reverberated through the tunnel.

Something tumbled into Mike's side, nearly knocking him down. He spun around with his gun and the Maglite, and had his finger on the trigger, about to squeeze, before he realized that the thing in his sights was the mop-headed Chicano kid. He froze, smelling his own sweat and fear.

"Don't walk slow on my account!" Twitch called. "The boy's got his own legs."

Mike turned and stumbled away from the niche of bones, fixing the beam of the flashlight on the ground and not looking at anything else. His heart raced at a thousand miles an hour and the rest of him felt numb.

The passage descended slowly, and as it dropped it opened up, the ceiling rising to twelve or fifteen feet over Mike's head and the walls as far apart. The space didn't make Mike feel any more comfortable. He stared at the pool of light, willing Chuy to leave him alone and hoping not to run into any more giant insects.

And then the passage abruptly ended.

Mike stopped, staring at the wall of yellowish brick and the iron door that barred his way. He pulled at the handle; it turned, but the door didn't open, and Mike saw that there was an antique-style keyhole in the handle's shadow.

"Mab's knuckles," Twitch commented as she and the kid joined him.

"What's the holdup?" Eddie hissed from the back. "This ain't no Sunday picnic, whatever Twitch might be whispering to the narcoleptic!" He caught up with the others. "Damn."

"Can you turn into a—" he almost said *fly*, "worm or something?" Mike asked Twitch.

"Even if I could," she said, "that door's iron."

CRASH!

"What does that mean?" he asked.

Everyone turned to look back. A flicker of colored light told Mike that the Hellhound had finally smashed through the trapdoor and was in the tunnel behind them.

"What it means," Eddie said, "is that we're in trouble."

He pumped his shotgun.

Chapter Six

Anyone got anything long and thin?" Mike asked, cold sweat bursting out all over his body. He regretted losing his switchblade in the melee at Butcher's.

"Not at the moment," Twitch snickered.

Mike felt himself blushing. "No, I mean like a bobby pin or a knife." It had been a while since Mike had picked a lock, but in his day he'd picked a lot of them. Jimmied open and hotwired a lot of cars, too, picked a pocket once or twice, and broken a lot of windows and legs. Besides, the keyhole was huge, a keyhole for an old-style warded lock rather than a modern tumbler, which probably meant that the lock was easy.

Eddie slapped a pocketknife into Mike's hand, still shaking from his encounter with the ghost.

"Thanks, Eddie," Mike said. While he snapped the blade open, he heard a ripping sound from the darkness where Eddie stood. He shone his light on the guitarist and saw Eddie strapping his Maglite to the underside of his shotgun with a strip of duct tape.

"You carry a lot of stuff in those pockets," he observed. The sweat on his body was drying and he started to shiver from the cold.

"Man of action has to be prepared," Eddie sniffed.

"Maybe you should MacGyver open the door."

"You MacGyver the door," Eddie chuckled. "I'm gonna MacGyver me a little Baal Zavuv."

"I don't think MacGyver used guns."

Eddie's eye skewed sideways and then he gritted his teeth and blinked. "I don't think MacGyver was ever on Hell's Ten Most Wanted list."

Eddie and Jim turned back to face the oncoming creatures and Mike knelt to look at the lock. "Can you hold the flashlight?" he asked Twitch.

"Son," Twitch said to the little kid, "hold the man's flashlight for him, will you, honey?"

The boy dutifully took the light and shone it on the keyhole, and Twitch went back to slapping Adrian's face.

Mike held the door handle down while he slipped the knife blade into the lock and probed around, feeling for the mechanism. "Where you from, kid?" he asked, and then, in case the boy's English wasn't so good, *"de dónde eres?"*

The kid shrugged.

Boom! The report of Eddie's shotgun was deafening inside the tunnel.

Mike worked faster. Eddie fired again and again. Twitch stroked Adrian's brow and murmur-sang a strange, modal-sounding lullaby. The mode didn't sound familiar, and Mike concentrated on the door, shutting the music out to avoid distraction.

"The rabbi was good to you, was he?"

The kid nodded. "He took me from the sisters," he said, in a high, piping voice. "I helped him around the temple. He taught me to walk in the path of knowledge."

"Oh, yeah?" Mike found a point inside the keyhole that resisted with some spring, but responded to pressure. He thought it might be the mechanism, and he worked on it. If he could get it to turn far enough, even if he couldn't rotate it all the way around, the door ought to open. "So you know the place pretty well? What's your name, so I can stop calling you 'kid'?"

"Rafael," the boy said.

The door in front of Mike face suddenly lit up with orange firelight marred by his own shadow, the source of the light behind him. With the light came a bellow that sounded inside the tunnel like the eruption of a volcano.

The boy trembled and stared up the passage at what must surely be the advancing Hellhound. Mike heard the rasp of metal-on-Hound-hide, and guessed that Jim had entered the fray. He also heard the buzzing of flies, and felt a little sick.

But he didn't see Chuy, and that was good. That was an improvement.

Adrian sat up. "What's going on?" he asked.

"What's always going on?" Twitch countered.

"Right." Adrian dug into his suit jacket as he climbed to his feet and came out with his machine pistol. "The more things change, and you know the rest."

Mike could hear the kid's knees knocking together. "Keep your eyes on me, Rafael," Mike urged him. "Did the rabbi give you that name?"

"The sisters did," Rafael said shyly. "But Rabbi Feldman thought it was a good sign."

"It is a good sign," Mike agreed. He didn't mean anything by it and the name meant nothing to him; he was just making small talk with the kid, to keep both the boy and himself distracted. His fingers were slippery from sweat and he had difficulty seeing through the fog of his own breath.

ROAR! Buzzzzzz!

Rat-tat-tat-tat-tat! Boom!

It sounded like a full-blown battle had broken out behind Mike, Adrian, and Eddie, supporting Jim. Mike resisted the urge to turn around and see how it was going.

"You can call me Rafi."

Click. The door handle popped down several extra inches and the door cracked open.

"What's behind the door, Rafi?"

Rafi shrugged. "This is as far as I've ever been."

Mike lurched to his feet, holding the door. "Well then," he said. "You'd better stand behind me, just in case."

Rafi stepped back, still shining the light on the door. Twitch moved to Mike's side, clubs in her hand. Mike pocketed the knife and palmed his pistol. He nodded to Twitch, then threw the door open.

On the other side waited cold, dark silence. A breeze cooled Mike's already chilled face even further, smelling faintly of some far-away waterhole. Behind him, the battle still raged, squealing and roars and bellows mixed in with the constant coughing of firearms and the gigantic buzzing of flies.

"Rafi," Mike said as gently as he could, "can I have the light?" He took the flashlight and shone it into the darkness ahead. "Stay close behind me," he told the boy.

He moved through the door. Beyond was a broad chamber, its walls of yellowish sandstone brick and its ceiling just over Mike's head. Facing him in the wall were three arched doorways. "Come on!" he hollered to the others, and stationed himself to the side so that he could see both the door he'd come through and the three new passageways. He didn't want anything sneaking up on him from behind.

Twitch pulled Rafi over to one side and perched next to the iron door, clubs raised over her head. "Come on!" she yelled.

Adrian backed through first, wiping sweat from his face and holstering his pistol. "That's me out of bullets then," he said glumly. He rummaged through pockets as he backed away from the door, pulling out bits of string, a stump of a candle, a little bone that might once have been part of a human finger.

Two Zvuvim buzzed in through the door after Adrian, and Twitch leaped to intercept them. She knocked one sideways and into the wall, where it hit with a *thud* and then slid to the ground making a sound that was part buzz and part whimper, but her swing at the second devil-fly missed. She whirled past the creature, overextended and vulnerable. It dove for her neck, buzzing like a power saw—

bang!

Mike splattered black dusty bits and goo all over the wall.

Twitch nodded quick thanks and resumed her position inside the door. Jim backed through next, ducking to get his head in under the doorframe. A Zavuv whizzed clacketing past his guard on the right, and as he stepped into the chamber Jim spun backward with his left hand snapping out in a roundhouse punch. He pummeled the Zavuv with his knuckles, pinning it against the wall.

It bit his forearm, drawing rivulets of bright red blood, but before Mike could get a clean shot, Jim punched the devil-fly in the center of its face with the hilt of his sword. Its eyes burst like Christmas tree ornaments hurled into a brick wall and sprayed thick, sour-smelling fluid on the floor.

Eddie stumbled back into the room, pulling his head down low in the collar of his army jacket like a turtle, and a spout of flame followed him. He tripped and fell flat, hitting the ground hard on his back, and aiming his shotgun at the shadow behind him. The huge black and gray Baal Zavuv rammed its head in through the doorway, its shoulders straining against the top of the frame. Tusks slobbered yellow and thousand-faceted eyes glittered like glass and the Baal bellowed, flies buzzing and swarming around it and erupting from its mouth.

Click.

Eddie's shotgun was out of shells.

Twitch slammed her batons on the Baal's eyes. They looked like glass, but they must be as hard as steel—she bounced off like she'd been kicked back. Jim stabbed at the Baal's neck from the other side; he drew blood, but the Baal didn't pull back.

Chingón. Mike started firing.

Bang! Bang! Bang! Click.

The Baal squealed, straining with its shoulders in the top of the doorframe like it might rip the wall open to get through. Zvuvim crawled through at its feet, buzzing ferociously. Mike thought he could taste his own heart in the back of this throat, even over the horrible rotting stench of the Baal and its horde of flies.

"Per Volcanum ignem mitto!" Adrian shouted.

A hot wind, full of fire and gold-red light, burst from the bit of candle and the glass lens Adrian held in his hand, slamming into the door. The Zvuvim caught in the blaze disappeared instantly into ash and were swept away. The Baal bellowed again and flailed its dagger-taloned hands, trying to bat away the stream of fire, or grapple it, and then the current swept the big demon out of the doorway.

Jim slammed the door shut.

The fire-wind turned off and Adrian staggered. Mike rushed to throw an arm around the shorter man and prop him up. "Good job," he complimented the organist.

"Yeah?" Adrian murmured, yawning and pinching himself. "I thought fight fire, et cetera …" He yawned again. "Damn this curse!"

"Stay awake!" Twitch snapped at him, and rapped him on the forehead with her baton.

"Ouch!"

In the outer passage, their demonic pursuers still raged. Mike eyed the door nervously, wondering how long it would hold.

Adrian shook himself and stood. "It's not my fault," he said.

"Nothing ever is," Eddie observed, standing and brushing himself off.

"What's the magic?" Mike asked Twitch. "Is it in the stick? Touching him on the head with the stick wakes him up?"

Twitch laughed. "I just like hitting him in the face," she said. "There's no magic. The poor idiot tries to cast spells, especially under pressure, and he gets suddenly very sleepy. You just do what you can to keep him awake."

"But what's the thing with the picnic?" Mike was puzzled. "The whole *we're all alone and it's nice here, Adrian* bit?"

"You're not my mama," Rafi said to Twitch.

"No," she agreed. "I'm too tired to be your mama anymore." She nodded at the iron door as it reverberated with another combined *roar-bellow-buzz*. "But I'm better than any of those things out there, aren't I?"

Rafi nodded.

Eddie limped over to join Jim, who stared at the three passages. Eddie shone his bayonet-flashlight over them by propping the gun in the crook of his arm as he reloaded it. "Does the boy know which door to take?"

"No," Mike and Rafi said together.

"But there's a breeze," Mike said, shuffling over to point at the passageway on the left, out of which he felt the air flowing. "See? This has to lead out."

"I ain't at all sure that where we want to get to is *out.*" Eddie and Jim looked at the passages further. "You see the glyphs, Jim?"

Jim nodded.

Mike looked to see what they were talking about, and realized that each passage had a symbol scratched over the top of it in the stone, and painted at the bottom with a white coloring, like clay. *Petroglyphs,* he thought they were called, though he'd never been a boy scout and had tried to avoid the deserts of Texas and New Mexico as much as he could. Each passage had a different symbol.

"A serpent," Eddie said. "A star. And what do you think that one might be?"

"A tree," Twitch guessed. It looked like a circle with a line coming down out of it, like a kid's stick-figure drawing of a tree.

"Does it mean anything?" Mike wanted to know.

Adrian shrugged. "They're all in Genesis, aren't they?"

"More Bible?" Mike groaned.

"Everything's *always* Bible in this band, Mikey," Twitch laughed lightly. "More's the pity for those of us who've never read it."

"You *could* call me *Mike,*" Mike suggested.

"I could."

"The star is the Host of Heaven," Adrian continued. "The serpent tempted Eve. And the tree is the Tree of Life."

"Knowledge," Eddie corrected him. "The knowledge of good and evil."

"Life," Adrian insisted, and deep inside Mike's fear-chilled and whisky-sodden head, a light bulb went on.

"Knowledge," he said. "We have to follow the path of knowledge."

"You read that in a fortune cookie?" Eddie asked.

Mike jerked a thumb at Rafi. "The boy told me. He's never been down here before, but Rabbi Feldman raised him to walk in the path of knowledge."

The boy nodded. "It's true."

Jim and Eddie locked eyes for a moment. Jim nodded, grabbed Mike's flashlight and started deliberately down the passage on the right, through the arch under the stylized tree. Adrian followed on the singer's heels.

"Let's just hope it *is* a tree," Twitch said impishly, "and not the famous lollipop of creation."

"There aren't any lollipops in Genesis," Eddie grumbled. "Creation or otherwise."

"Really?" Twitch grinned. "That's a shame. I like a good lollipop."

Something heavy slammed against the iron door and it groaned and buckled in response.

"Get moving," Eddie ordered, pumping his shotgun. "I have the rear."

Twitch jogged up the passage, followed by Mike and the boy Rafi, who ran with them now without anyone holding his hand. Mike let himself get distracted by the sight of Twitch's horse's tail bouncing from side to side like a tassel fixed to her leather pants as she ran, until he remembered that whatever she was, she wasn't quite a woman—not *exactly*. For that matter, he wondered now whether the tail really was attached to her pants, or what precisely he would see if she weren't wrapped in leather and spikes.

He cleared his throat and shook his head.

"What's with … the tree?" he huffed and puffed to Eddie, who jogged two paces behind him, and in the light of whose flashlight Mike shuffled along. His heart pounded, and almost immediately he got a stitch in his side. He needed to drop some weight and get into shape.

Couldn't quit drinking, of course.

"It's a marker," Eddie said. "Like a code. Like blood on the doorposts on Passover. Let him who has ears hear."

"A tree?" Mike followed Jim and the others ahead, through a series of quick turns. The passages all looked the same to him, carved sandstone bricks like he was inside one of the pyramids of Egypt, and he had to trust that Jim was on the right track.

"The tree of knowledge of good and evil," Eddie said. "The tree that is the candlestick that is the woman that is the river, et cetera. Not to sound too much like Adrian."

"All that stuff is the same thing?" Mike tried to clarify. "You look for a tree or a river or a light, you're going to see them all over the place."

"Context matters," Eddie said. "And symbols matter. You live long enough, Mike, you realize that there's a whole world underneath the world that we see, and its symbols that tell you how to get around it."

"Who *are* you guys?" Mike asked. "I mean, really?"

Eddie chuckled. "That's a lot of story you're asking about," he said.

A distant bellow echoed through the labyrinth, and Mike wondered if the demons had broken through the iron door. "Can they follow us by smell?"

"The Hound can. The Baal, too, maybe, if our smell is distinctive enough."

"What does that mean?"

"It means through a crowded city, maybe not, but through a labyrinth where almost no one ever goes, yeah, the Baal Zavuv might be able to sniff us out."

Mike squeezed the grip of his pistol once to reassure himself that he still had it. "You're not a rock band."

"Sure we are," Eddie said. "We're a hard working rock band, too. It's how we pay our way, limited engagements, strictly cash. Hell, we're even *good,* in our fashion. New name for the band every gig, of course, so we're harder to track, and that makes it impossible to build up a fan base, as does the fact that we can't record."

Mike rattled down stone steps. "And what's with the tambourine?"

Eddie was quiet for a moment. "Everyone in this band," he finally said, "has a bone to pick with Satan. The tambourine is mine."

Mike almost laughed out loud. "Do you have any idea how stupid that sounds?" he asked. "What does that even mean?"

"It means I'm the best damn tambourine player in the whole damn world," Eddie said gruffly. "Bar none, nobody else is even close."

Mike remembered the agent at Butcher's and the pleading look in his eyes. "I still don't get it."

"What I wanted to be was the world's best guitar player," Eddie said. "I was okay, starting to make a name for myself in some of the bars around Chicago, but I needed to get much better, and much faster than I could on my own. I needed it for my kids, you understand? For my family. It wasn't an ego thing, I didn't want screaming fans or limousines or coke to snort off the backsides of expensive hookers. So I did like all the songs said. I let a hoodoo woman take me down to the crossroads."

Mike stumbled and almost fell. "You mean you sold your soul to the devil?"

"Keep running!" Eddie was quiet again. "Yeah," he continued, "only I screwed up."

Mike said nothing to that. He'd screwed up plenty, himself.

"I told Old Scratch—or his errand boy, anyway, you hardly ever get to meet the poobah himself in person, not on Earth and not in Hell, either—that I wanted to be the world's best rock and roll *musician*. Damn me, if I'd just said *guitar player* it would have been all right. Instead, I sold my soul and just about lost my sanity, and all I got for it is that I'm the world's most amazing genius at rock and roll *tambourine*."

Mike gulped. "Lost your sanity?" he was ahead of Eddie, and after the story he'd just heard, didn't feel really comfortable looking back.

"Out of my left eye," Eddie said, in a voice that sounded like gravel and razor wire, "I see Hell. All the time. And when I sleep, I dream my death."

"Mierda," Mike muttered. He thought of Chuy and shuddered.

"One thing you'll learn quick in this band," Eddie added somberly, "if you ain't learned it already, is that Satan's got game."

Abruptly they caught up to the others. At a final arch, the labyrinth ended, and they found themselves standing on a rough sandstone shelf under an immense stone overhang. Off to their right, Mike could see what looked like a dark-walled canyon, its depths choked with boulders and desert scrub, and a few winking stars peeping down on it from above. The light of the stars and moon was silvery and faint, but it gave Mike more ability to see than he'd had since they'd slammed the trapdoor shut in the synagogue, and he was grateful for it.

In front of them, below the overhang, lay a long strip of packed sand. At the far end of the sandbar, maybe as much as half a mile away, was a brick building. It looked like a cube that narrowed as it rose, like a ziggurat or a pyramid with its tip knocked off.

Mike smelled water.

"That's gotta be it," Eddie guessed, shining his flashlight on the stone structure.

From within the labyrinth, Mike heard the squealing of the Baal Zavuv and the roaring of the Hellhound.

"Let's not stop here," he said, and followed Jim, who was already trotting toward the pyramid.

Chapter Seven

Jim and Eddie both shone their flashlights around the overhanging stone as they walked, and Mike looked up. The moon- and star-light didn't reach the stone, but what he saw in the splashes of Maglite beam took his breath away.

The entire underside of the cliff was scratched and scarred with petroglyphs. Some formed distinct scenes, and at a walking pace Mike couldn't really figure out what was being portrayed. There were definitely monsters and battles and big beasties inside cages, and some of the creatures carved into the stone were reminiscent of the dragons and angels he'd seen in the tapestries in the synagogue above. He wondered how old the synagogue was, and then he wondered if it really was a synagogue. There was even one picture that looked like an angel riding a dragon underneath a river of water, all done in ancient stick-figure style.

There was writing, too, definitely. Mike was no expert, and he didn't recognize the alphabet, but there was row after row of what could only be words and letters. Some of it, he thought, looked suspiciously like Egyptian hieroglyphs, maybe a little stylized. Zig-zaggy lines, dogs lying down, people with their arms raised over their heads. Someone, a long, long time ago, had spent a lot of time and effort carving this rock.

Below all the writing, greenery clung to the rock, which reflected the beams of the flashlight like it was wet.

Jim stopped at the base of the brick pyramid and the others caught up. The pyramid was bigger than it had looked from the labyrinth exit. A *kiva,* Mike thought they called these things when they were in old Pueblo or the Anasazi ruins. Only kivas were small, like sweat lodges. This was a super-kiva. If Donald Trump built a kiva, it would look like this.

"What is that stuff?" Mike panted, and pointed at the ceiling.

Eddie ran his flashlight across the overhang again. "Writing," he said. "And pictures."

"No kidding." Mike's side ached. "But I mean … who wrote it?"

"Someone who's dead now." The guitar player ran his light over the structure. A sort of ladder, consisting of a single straight tree trunk with rungs lashed crosswise to it, leaned up against the side of the building, not quite reaching the top. The wood looked as dried out as could be and the lashings were made of dry wiry grass. Mike resolved not to trust the ladder with his weight, no matter what. Under the light's beam he could see that the sides weren't totally sheer anyway, but rose steeply in narrow steps. The super-kiva was climbable.

Jim kept walking, around the base of the pyramid, shining his flashlight at the ground and inspecting it.

"Not necessarily," Twitch contradicted him.

"Looks similar to proto-Eblaite," Adrian squinted. "Or Reformed Egyptian. My guess is it's one of the Primals, though of course you can write with any alphabet."

"You can?" Mike asked.

"Yeah," Eddie agreed. "This is the place."

"What do you mean, one of the Primals?" Mike felt dizzier with each new rush of information, though he was well through the looking glass at this point and no longer questioned anything he was told, not really. With the Hellhound and Baal Zavuv on his tail, skepticism didn't seem likely to contribute to his survival. "What place is this?"

"The Primals are the three original languages spoken on this planet at the moment of the Fall of Adam," Adrian said. "Really, they're dialects of the same language, but you say potato … you know."

Mike groped to understand. "What do you mean … like, Latin?" he asked.

Eddie laughed sourly. "Latin is a late arrival on the scene. Latin is practically *modern*. You can study Latin in *high school.*"

"I mean Angelic," Adrian said, "and Infernal, and Adamic."

"You speak these languages?"

Adrian chuckled. Mike thought his laugh sounded a little condescending, and if he hadn't been so exhausted, he might have bristled a little. "Oh, no. No human being has been able to speak or understand the Primals for thousands of years. Not since the Tower of Babel. We're not *capable* of it, not since we were cursed."

"Nor are *we*," Twitch added. "For entirely different reasons."

"We?" Mike fumbled. "Who's *we*?"

"As for what this place is," Eddie said, "this is the place we came looking for. This is Dudael." He cleared his throat and spoke again in his recitative chanting voice. "And the Lord said to Raphael: bind Azazel hand and foot and throw him into the darkness! And he made a hole in the desert which was in Dudael and cast him there; he threw on top of him rugged and sharp rocks. And he covered his face in order that he may not see light; and in order that he may be sent into the fire on the great day of judgment."

"That in the Bible again?" Mike asked. He remembered Adrian had said that Azazel was Satan.

"Nah," Eddie said, "but it should be."

Mike looked up at the overhanging stone, so vast that the super-kiva was almost inside a cave. "That's a rugged rock," he agreed, "and I guess the sun hasn't ever shone inside here." Then he made another connection. "Raphael!"

"A good sign," the boy chirped. He wouldn't meet Mike's eyes and just stood there with his hands in his pockets. Well, no wonder, the poor kid was certainly having the worst day of his life, worse than anything he could ever have imagined.

Like the day Chuy died had been, for Mike.

Then another thought occurred to him and he jumped back from the brick building. "But—Satan! Azazel!"

Eddie chuckled. "Don't worry, His Lowness broke out of this particular hoosegow ages ago."

"So it's safe?"

"Oh, hell no. But you're not going to meet Satan today."

From back inside the labyrinth, Mike heard the roar of the Hellhound and the bellow of the Baal Zavuv. They sounded closer than before.

"Unless you die," Adrian added. "You do, after all, have the Hand on you."

"Thanks," Mike said, and shuddered. "That's cheerful."

"That's our Adrian," Twitch grinned. "A little ray of sunshine. Et cetera."

Mike almost chuckled at Twitch's jab. "Now what?" he asked.

"Now," Eddie told him, "you help us look for a bit of hoof."

"Like a horse's hoof?" Mike looked at Twitch, without meaning to.

"More like a goat's," Eddie said. "A really *big* goat."

Adrian looked up at the overhang, pressing the little glass lens to his eye. "No, there are plenty of wards on the stone here, but they're all broken. We're on a fool's errand. If it was here, just lying in the sand, Satan would have found it long ago."

"Unless there's some other reason Lucifer can't see it." Eddie ambled off, scanning the ground.

"I don't get it," Mike said. He stumbled after Eddie, and the boy Rafael trailed in his wake. Eddie moved slowly around the base of the building, shining his light on the sand and scuffing at it with the toe of his boot. Behind the building, in Eddie's light, Mike now saw that the water trickling down the back of the overhang gathered into a channel, lined with brick, and flowed into a hole in the wall of the kiva. Mike thought hard as he walked, trying to stitch the pieces together in his mind. "It can't be a real goat's hoof. Are you telling me that we're here looking for *a piece of Satan?*"

"In fact, I don't think I did tell you that," Eddie said. "But it's still true. I'm glad you're paying attention. You're much more likely to survive if you do."

"Huevos."

"Pretty much."

Rafi closed in behind Mike and grabbed his free hand. "But … how long has it been here?" Mike asked. "How … how do you know it's here? How … how…?"

Eddie continued moving and examining the ground. The super-kiva, Mike realized as he stood directly under it, was much bigger than he had at first thought. It really was like one of the pyramids, cropped at the top and uprooted into nowhere, New Mexico.

"It's been here since his escape," Eddie said matter-of-factly. "Call it six thousand years, in round numbers. No one realized it because, naturally, His Lowness wanted to keep the vulnerability a secret. Jim found out it was here, back when Jim was in Hell's good graces. Or rather, its bad graces."

"Vulnerability?"

"You heard about voodoo dolls?"

"I watch TV."

Eddie snorted. "Imagine the possibilities."

Mike did, and felt troubled. What could someone achieve who had the power to harm, or maybe kill, Satan? The blackmail opportunities seemed vast. And what if someone with the hoof could do more than that? What if he could actually *control* the Prince of Darkness? Mike gulped. "How can it still be here after all that time? And how can we possibly find a bit of hoof?"

Jim whistled, fingers in his mouth, and Eddie looked up at him. Jim waved an arm at the building and started marching toward it. Eddie turned to look at the brick too, pulling at it with his fingers to test its stability.

Mike heard another Hellhound roar. Eddie seemed not to have noticed.

"It can still be here," Eddie explained, "if for thousands of years, a long line of canny old Hebrew priests has been carefully watching over it, keeping it hidden with wards of obfuscation and other tricks."

"Hebrews in New Mexico?" Mike scoffed. "Thousands of years ago?"

"Those guys get around," Eddie shook his head. "You'd be surprised. And I *don't* expect you and me to find it." He twisted off his flashlight, let the shotgun hang down from his shoulder and started to climb up the side of the building.

"Then why are we wasting our time?"

"I expect *Jim* to find it," Eddie continued. "He's got something of a connection with it, after all. And if it isn't him, it'll be Adrian. Using voodoo doll principles, if he can manage to do it without taking a surprise nap."

Mike gave the boy Rafi a boost, shoving him up the side of the pyramid. He scrambled like a monkey, and Mike followed like a bull, plodding on all fours up the side of the brick. To his surprise, it bore his weight without crumbling or shifting. The solidity of the brick made him wonder a bit about the story Eddie was telling him; he didn't think the super-kiva could possibly be six thousand years old.

Eddie and Rafi were both between him and the curtain of starlight over the canyon below, so they were silhouettes to him, scaling the side of the pyramid much surer and faster than Mike could.

"Why wouldn't the Hebrew priests give the hoof back?" Mike asked, puffing.

"To Satan?"

"I mean to … to Heaven." Mike scratched his head. "I guess that's not really giving it *back*, is it?"

Eddie shrugged. "Maybe they did. Or maybe Heaven wouldn't want it back, like trying to give the White House a chunk of radioactive waste, or a block of kryptonite to Superman. Or maybe Heaven *would* want it, but the priests were too smart to give it to them. Some of this stuff is just beyond me, and I sort of figure it always will be. I'm a practical man, with limited objectives."

"Why would holding it back make any sense?" Mike asked. "I mean, if it's like a voodoo doll, couldn't Heaven use the bit of hoof to trap Satan again? Or have power over him, somehow?"

"I guess that's my point," Eddie stopped to wipe sweat from his forehead. "Maybe it's better for everyone if Heaven *can't* do that. Maybe it's better if there's an opposition, even if it's …" he hesitated, "ugly. But I might be talking out my backside, sometimes I can't tell."

"Don't you want to get rid of Hell?" Mike asked, remembering Eddie's wandering eye and the grim sound of his voice when the guitar player had said he saw Hell out of his left eye perpetually.

"No," Eddie shook his head slowly and spoke with quiet determination. "I don't want to go to Hell myself, but I sure think some people belong there."

All three of them reached the top of the pyramid at the same time as Jim. Rafi and Eddie looked tired and Mike felt exhausted; Jim looked totally unfazed by the climb. Adrian and Twitch still stood at the bottom, Adrian staring at the brick building through his lens and Twitch talking to him.

"What do you mean," Mike asked uneasily, looking from Eddie to Jim and back, "when you say that Jim used to be in *Hell's good graces?*"

Eddie turned to look at Jim; Jim nodded.

"It all has to do with the reason that the rebel angels fell," Eddie explained slowly. He started reciting again: "They took wives unto themselves, and everyone chose one woman for himself, and they began to go unto them. And they taught them magical medicine, incantations, the cutting of roots, and taught them plants. And the women became pregnant and gave birth to great giants."

The stone overhang felt very close, and loomed over Mike's head like it wanted to crush him; the ground below felt very far away, and seemed to be spinning. "The angels had children." He took a deep breath. "With human women."

"Oh, yes."

"Jim's not a giant." Mike gulped, and then glanced quickly at the big Viking-looking singer who loomed over him. "Well, sort of, he is."

"Sort of, he is," Eddie agreed. "And sort of, so is Twitch."

"Twitch?"

Something silver flashed in the corner of Mike's vision. Mike only saw it for a split second, but if pressed, he would have sworn he'd seen a big silver bird, like a hawk or an eagle, swooping to alight on top of the pyramid. Only the eagle, he would have sworn, had a long tassel flying in the wind behind it, like the tail of a horse.

He turned, and Twitch was standing there.

"Yes, Mikey?" she said.

"What *are* you?" he asked. He was so thrown off by the entire conversation, he barely noticed her calling him 'Mikey.' Rafi grabbed his hand and squeezed it.

"Haven't you figured it out yet?" she chuckled, her white tail swishing merrily back and forth. "Some would say I'm one of the fair folk."

"Descended from rebel angels?"

Twitch snorted. "Oh, that's what some of the *Fallen* say, but they say that about practically *everyone*. Everyone who's anyone, at least. Who knows, really? Semyaz goes around tooting his horn that he's Osiris's father, but you don't see Osiris sending the crusty old bastard Father's Day cards, do you?"

"I don't," Mike admitted. "But I'm new to all this."

"Trust me," Twitch elbowed Mike confidentially in the ribs, "he doesn't."

"But what do *you* say?"

"I'm Mab's child," Twitch said lightly. "By Oberon. Whose children *they* might be, they've never told me and I don't care."

"Well how else do you explain it?" Mike asked.

"Explain what?"

"Uh … explain *fairies*? That's what we're talking about, right?" Mike's head was spinning, and he tried to clutch tight to the thread of the conversation. "You're a fairy, aren't you? How do you explain that?"

Twitch snorted. "Explain that I *exist*? How do you explain that *you* exist? Do you have an explanation, or just a bunch of guesses? And since when did everything have to be explained, anyway? I swear, the Enlightenment ruined you humans forever."

"I don't know." Mike felt defensive. He wasn't sure what enlightenment even had to do with anything; didn't that mean people in California sitting in the Lotus position and burning incense? "Stuff should make sense, I guess."

"For that matter, how does Eddie here explain that Jim and I are so different, if we're supposed to be cousins?"

"Different?"

"Do you see Jim changing shape? Do you see him burning at the touch of iron? Or do you see me commanding the legionaries of Hell and biting my tongue all the time for fear my dad will hear me?"

"You're both immortal," Eddie pointed out.

"And you and the chimpanzees both have opposable thumbs!" Twitch snapped. "Do I go about telling everyone you're related?"

"I might be related to chimpanzees," Eddie said, "for pretty much exactly that reason."

"Jim's immortal?" Mike asked.

"Well, he doesn't get old, anyway," Eddie modified his words. "We think he can probably be killed."

"Probably?"

"Well, you never really know until you try, do you?" Twitch pointed out. "And if it was you, would you want to experiment?"

"How old is he?" Mike looked at Jim.

"I've been hearing about him for a good long time," Twitch said.

"He once told me he learned to fence from Cyrano de Bergerac. So what is that, at least four hundred years?" Eddie shrugged. "He might have been pulling my leg."

Mike wasn't sure, but he thought Cyrano de Bergerac might be one of the Three Musketeers. Or the fourth musketeer, maybe, the new guy that got into all the fights. He felt disoriented and afraid, and then Jim put a hand on his shoulder.

The hand calmed him somehow. And in the shadow, poorly lit by reflected light from the stars above the canyon and from the two flashlights, Mike thought he saw Jim smile. It was enough.

He took a deep breath. "Okay. What now?"

Puffing, Adrian reached the top of the pyramid. The space they all occupied was a flat platform, roughly ten feet to a side. "There's a way in," Adrian huffed. "I can't see it from the ground, but it's up here."

"Everybody step back," Eddie said. "Without, you know, falling off. Look for something that will get us inside."

"It won't be a doorbell!" Adrian snapped. "There are wards."

Mike shuffled back to the edge of the pyramid. From the top, it reminded him not of Egyptian pyramids nor of Anasazi kivas, but of old Maya ruins he'd seen on TV documentaries, late at night and drunk. The connection didn't put his mind at ease at all—he had a dim memory that, according to those same documentaries, the Maya had sacrificed humans on top of their pyramids. Tied them into balls and rolled them down the sides or something. He looked down the slopes of the pyramid into darkness, sweating and nervous.

Rafi took his free hand.

"Thanks, kid," he said.

"What do you see?" Eddie asked.

Adrian stood at the other end of the square platform, his lens held up to his eye. He swept his head back and forth, examining the pyramid. "This thing is warded to high Heaven," he said. "Forgive the pun."

"What kind of wards?" Eddie asked.

"Sealing, for one, and strengthening." Adrian blinked through his lens. "I think the top of the pyramid itself is the door," he said slowly, "only those wards will have to be undone. And that's complicated by a gnarly-looking ward of entrapment."

"Should I go back to the van and get your jammies?" Eddie mocked him.

"Making fun of me doesn't lift the curse," Adrian growled. He was still looking through the lens. "And under all that there are serious wards of obfuscation and silence." He looked up at Jim. "*Serious* wards. Someone wants something inside this kiva to stay hidden, and I'd guess anything inside is undetectable … to anyone."

"This might be it," Twitch suggested. "About time."

Jim nodded.

"Better get going," Eddie pushed the spellcaster along. "You have everything you need?"

Adrian tucked his lens away and grinned. "Of course. I live by the Boy Scout slogan: be prepared."

"That's the *motto,*" Eddie rumbled. "Get on it, then."

Adrian took two pieces of colored chalk from inside his jacket and stepped out onto the platform. He knelt, to begin to draw—

and Rafi suddenly yanked on Mike's arm, hauling him sideways and off balance—

the kid grabbed Mike's gun as they crossed paths in mid-air—

Bang! bang! Adrian tumbled back—

and Mike hit the brick hard, bouncing and tumbling down the side of the pyramid. He threw his arms and legs out, slapping at the brick as the world spun about him and catching himself halfway down, his shoulder jammed up against the top of the super-kiva's pole-ladder. When he stared up again past his own toes and toward the top of the pyramid, he saw Rafi, pointing Mike's pistol at Jim.

"The Hound and the Baal are minor servants of Hell," Rafi said, "and nearly mindless." His voice boomed and echoed, like

Jim's had when singing in the bar. He didn't sound like a little kid anymore, not at all, and the giant voice was all wrong, coming out of a kid in baggy jeans and high tops. "They don't know about the hoof, and I won't let them learn. All they want is *you* … *Jim*, if that's what you want to call yourself … and as far as I'm concerned, they can have you."

At that moment, Mike heard the squealing bellow and a thunder-like roar.

He craned his head around and saw the Hellhound finally burst from the mouth of the labyrinth, the flames of its body lighting the swarming cloud of flies and the Baal Zavuv that followed closely on its tail.

CHAPTER EIGHT

ow did I not see you?" Eddie demanded, staring at the little
kid.

"He's not an Infernal is how," Twitch guessed. "He's
something else."

Mike heard the words, but it took a moment for them to sink
in. He couldn't turn, and he couldn't stand, so he was letting his
body do a slow half-somersault over his own shoulder, grunting
and straining in discomfort, to try to get upright. The ladder
helped—he gripped it with both hands and hoped it wouldn't
shatter. He wondered how sturdy six-thousand-year-old wood
could possibly be, and as he asked himself the question, the grasses
holding the top rung in place snapped. His somersault rolled
downward and forward faster than he meant it, a piece of wood
came off in his hands, and he scrambled with fingers and toes to
keep his grip.

"I'm not an Infernal," Rafi agreed. The little kid's voice
boomed against the overhang and echoed loud in Mike's ears. It
seemed deeper now.

"Rabbi Feldman?" Eddie ventured.

Mike got himself upright and looked around. He found himself
standing high on the side of the super-kiva, the balls of his feet and
his toes wedged onto a shelf barely big enough to hold them. Rafi

had his pistol, which left Mike a spare clip, a pocketful of shells, and Eddie's pocketknife. And a chunk of wood the size of a fireplace log.

The Baal Zavuv squealed. Mike could hear the buzzing of the cloud of giant flies.

"Getting warmer."

"You're Raphael," Twitch said. "The angel himself. There's no line of Hebrew priests in Dudael, there never was. Just you, like the book says, keeping vigil here by yourself for thousands of years."

"Very good." The voice was way too big for the little kid, and sort of creepy coming out of his mouth. The gun was too big for him too, and as he waved it at Eddie it looked like a cannon in his hands. "Drop your gun," he ordered the guitar player. "Unless you want to go to Hell right now."

Eddie dropped the shotgun to the top of the kiva, a sour expression on his face.

Jim strained forward at the shoulders, like he wanted to go all Hulk on the guy, shred his shirt and then rip the kid to pieces, but he didn't. He just stood in place and left his sword where it was, hanging on his belt.

Mike was painfully aware of the Hellhound and the Baal Zavuv, racing across the sand toward them all. He didn't know how long they had, but it wasn't minutes—it was seconds at best. He forced himself to keep his back turned to the approaching demons and to keep dragging himself up the side of the kiva, one brick at a time.

Maybe, he thought, *I should have shot myself after all.*

"I guess you've been switching bodies over the years," Eddie grumped. "Makes sense. Couldn't have people seeing too many full-on fire-of-Heaven manifestations, even out here in the ass end of New Mexico."

"When the Baal spiked you, you already had a new host body, and you just made the jump." Twitch laughed. "I guess it's better to be a little kid than to be an old man full of hatching fly eggs."

The Hound roared.

"It seemed like a random event," Rafael nodded, "and it was. They didn't recognize me and they weren't after my charge. They were hunting you. At first I thought I'd just have to wait out the flies, but then you showed up. Now I'll give you to the Hound and the Baal, and they'll be on their way."

"Or Jim could say *boo*," Eddie countered, "and this little tussle would suddenly have the attention of half the Infernal Council."

"Jim goes back to Hell either way," the little boy said. The light from Eddie's dropped shotgun shone up off the floor into his face, making his grin look demonic. Mike inched a few more bricks up the side of the super-kiva, sweat freezing him. "I'm betting *hope* will keep his mouth shut."

"Heaven's secret weapon," Twitch said grimly. "Pandora's curse."

Mike hefted the wood in his hand, wondering how close he'd have to get before he could club Rafi with it. The thought made him hesitate—Rafi looked a little too much like Chuy for Mike's comfort. Plus, he was just a kid … or he *looked* like a kid, anyway. What kind of man hit kids?

Mike felt a wave of guilt and shame.

"Don't you think Heaven would be interested in getting its hands on Jim?" Eddie suggested. The Hound and the Baal were close enough that Mike could hear the buzzing of flies and the *whumph-whumph-whumph* of big demon claws in the sand even over the hammering of his own out-of-control heart. "He'd be one hell of a bargaining chip, forgive the pun."

"Don't flatter yourself," Rafi laughed. "Heaven doesn't want Jim. Heaven doesn't want any of you."

ROAR! Graaaaaraaagh!

Jim opened his mouth like he was about to speak—

"Unless—" Rafi said. He looked sly and devious.

No more time. Mike took aim at the kid's chest and threw the wood at him.

Rafi took one slight step forward and the throw missed—

Rafi turned and grinned at Mike, and Mike's heart sank—

Plunk!

Adrian rolled over onto his back, both hands out in front of him, and Mike heard a high-pitched *chatta-chatta-chatta* sound. Rafi's arms and legs danced spastically, he dropped the gun and fell to the platform.

"Taser, bitch!" Adrian shouted.

"Eddie!" Twitch yelled. The fairy moved like a blur, her batons appearing in her hands (Mike wondered where she kept them—they seemed to be in her hands when she wanted them, and then they vanished when she didn't), and as Mike lumbered up to the top of the platform, she met him, shoving his pistol into his hands and then passing him, headed down.

"Watch the kid!" Eddie shouted, then shook his head. "I mean, the archangel!" Then the guitarist slid down the edge of the kiva on Jim's heels, shotgun blasting at the cloud of incoming Zvuvim.

Adrian handed the taser to Mike and brushed himself off. Adrian held the second flashlight, and in its beam Mike saw that filaments ran from the little gray rubberized box in his hand to darts in Rafi's chest. The boy was sitting up, slowly, as if his muscles were cramped.

"Don't talk, you slimy bastard!" Adrian barked at the little kid. "You talk, Mike here zaps you!"

"Yeah." Mike tried to sound tough. He tried to remember that the little kid was really an immortal archangel, and had just thrown him off the top of the kiva like Mike was an unwanted kitten.

"Also," Adrian told Mike matter-of-factly, "zap him if you need to keep him under control so you can get off a shot at the bugs coming in. For that matter, you ought to zap him every once in a while for fun." Adrian grabbed the taser in Mike's hands and pressed down on the button with his thumb.

Chatta-chatta-chatta.

Rafi thumped back onto the platform, heels kicking and head bouncing around.

Boom! Boom! Jim kept the Hellhound at bay, stabbing down from the side of the super-kiva as the beast lunged at him with its forepaws. Eddie rained shotgun blasts at the Zvuvim swarming around his friend. Mike couldn't see the Baal Zavuv, or Twitch, and that made him nervous.

"And don't forget," Adrian said, "he's an archangel. Don't trust him for a second, those guys are in on it."

"In on what?"

"*It.*" Adrian waved his hand around vaguely at the world. "Everything. Believe me, Mike, the joke's on us."

Mike looked down at the taser. "How many zaps does this thing's battery hold?" he asked.

Adrian shrugged, holding his lens up to his eye again. "I've juiced it up a little," he said, "tinkerer that I am. In theory, that should mean bigger shocks and more of them. In practice, well, don't count your chickens, et cetera."

"You saying the taser might fall asleep when I try to use it?" Mike grinned.

"Hey!" Adrian barked. "Don't you start!" He swept the top of the platform with the flashlight beam, then started to chuckle. "Everybody thinks he's a comedian. Even the monkey on the bass."

Rafael opened his mouth to say something. Remembering Adrian's warning, Mike thumbed the shock button on the taser and sent the kid into another round of spasms. "I kinda feel weird," he said. "I mean, I'm standing here tasering an angel. At least I think I am."

Adrian chalked a straight line along one edge of the super-kiva platform, jogging it into a lightning bolt every couple of feet. "Don't feel weird. Feel proud. Get some good licks in for the whole species."

"On *angels*? I mean, *joy to the world*?"

"Yeah, joy to the world, exactly." Adrian squinted through his lens and switched to a different color of chalk. "Joy to the world, *whether you want it or not*. Can't leave the poor shepherds well enough alone. Can't let Balaam just ride his donkey in peace. Can't just let people live decent lives and be happy, can they? Nope, Heaven meddles. Heaven is a bunch of busybodies. Heaven wants to make everybody *better*."

Mike shook his head, confused. "But what I really mean is that I can't believe it works on him. I mean, he's an angel."

"Yeah, well," Adrian exhaled slowly as he drew a long arc with his chalk. "He's in a body now, isn't he? Anything with a body, you can taser it. Remember Legion and the pigs at Capernaum?"

"No."

"Ha. Well, they can drown, too, when they've chained themselves to human bodies. Doesn't destroy them, of course, but it messes them up and they don't like it. I'm not sure, but I think it's kind of like getting your horse knocked out from under you if you're a cowboy." Adrian stood up, and Mike realized he'd forgotten something.

"Didn't you get shot?" he asked. Adrian looked unscathed.

The organist snorted. "Ward of shielding," he said, as if that explained it. "Stung like the dickens, but didn't break the skin. Stupid angel's been out here on his own in the boondocks so long, he's forgotten how the game is played."

The fight below sounded like a storm, shotgun blasts and the terrifying bellows of demons.

Mike risked a look around and found Twitch. She was on the ground on the far side of the kiva from Jim and Eddie, in horse form, kicking with hind legs at the Baal Zavuv. The big grey and black demon bellowed and squealed and swiped at her with both hands, and there was bright red blood on the horse's flanks. A cloud of Zvuvim buzzed around, clutching with shiny steel mandibles, and Twitch bit back with enormous white horsey teeth.

Mindful of the archangel he held prisoner, Mike squeezed the taser's shock button with his left thumb. At the same time, he raised his semi-automatic in his other hand and squeezed off a handful of rounds, *bang! bang! bang!* pulverizing several Zvuvim in mid-air and even, he thought, landing a shot or two on the big tusked fly-pig-demon thing. It didn't seem fazed by the bullets.

Adrian set the flashlight down on the edge of the platform. "Now," the wizard told him, putting away the chalk and dusting his hands off against each other, "you got the most important job of the evening."

"Yeah?" Mike asked, keeping an eye on Twitch in her strange, circling and kicking dance-fight against the Baal. "What's that, then?"

"You gotta keep me awake."

That got Mike's attention. "How do I do that?" he asked. "There's something Twitch does with her voice, but I don't—"

"Yeah, she has Glamour."

Mike felt relieved that he wasn't the only one. "Yeah," he admitted, "I guess I think she's glamorous, too."

"Doesn't always work. Nothing *always* works. Just—look, keep an eye on me, and do what you gotta do. Pinch me, shout, hold me up, whatever. Best you don't shoot me with the taser, though."

"That's a nasty curse," Mike said, remembering Adrian's earlier insistence on the fact of his being cursed, and not just naturally narcoleptic.

"And keep an eye on Raphael," Adrian added, rolling up the crisped and burned sleeves of his suit jacket and stepping to the edge of the platform. "Heaven's up to something here. I don't like it."

"Heaven help us," Mike ventured with a grin. "Et cetera?"

"Not very damn likely," Adrian snorted, then turned to his incantation. *"Per Wepwawet Mercuriumque,"* he started chanting, waving his arms. His eyes grew distant in concentration. He was focusing so hard he looked like he was in a trance.

Mike looked away from Adrian just in time to see a big Zavuv that had gotten past Eddie and raced in his direction. He pointed his pistol at it and squeezed the trigger.

Click.

"Huevos."

No time to duck, and barely any time to move at all. The fly rushed for his head, metal mandibles clicking like scythes hungry for the harvest—

Mike swung his fist backhand, pistol-whipping the Zavuv across both eyes—

crash! the demon-fly's eyes shattered and sour, reeking fluid like pus sprayed all over Mike. He flinched, and the Zavuv's body collided with his shoulder, knocking him back two steps and making him teeter on the edge of the super-kiva's platform for long, dizzying seconds. When he had windmilled back into balance, the Zavuv was gone, its body indistinguishable in the carpet of shredded black demon-flesh scattered across the sand around the pyramid.

Mike looked around the super-kiva, checking in on the rest of the band. Jim and the Hound were so close together in their struggle they might have been wrestling. Eddie swung with the butt of his shotgun at the flies swarming around him, ducking and trying to reload. Mike grabbed for his spare clip, meaning to reload his own weapon and clear out some of the Zvuvim assailing Eddie.

"Mike," he heard a voice say.

It was a sweet voice, so sweet he had to listen. It might have been a woman's voice, it was so sweet, but Mike didn't think it was. The voice didn't turn him on, but it warmed his heart and made him feel thrilled.

"Mike," the voice said again, "we can be on the same side."

Some part of Mike's brain knew that he still stood on top of a half-pyramid underneath a rock overhang somewhere in the middle of New Mexico, surrounded by minor minions of Hell and assigned to keep a narcoleptic wizard from nodding off, but that wasn't what he saw. He saw hills, green and rolling under a carpet of flowers, and beyond them a forest and the sea and overhead a brilliant blue sky and all around were fruit trees and friendly wild creatures and birds and butterflies and he smelled warm pollen on the gentle breeze and there wasn't a cloud in sight. And there on the hillock with him stood his good friend Rafael, the little kid who was so funny and brave and charming, and he smiled at Mike.

"Mike," he said, "let's do some good together." And when Rafael said it, Mike wasn't sure exactly what he had in mind, but he really wanted to cooperate.

"Do some good," he mumbled. "Do some good, and go to Heaven."

"Heaven loves those who do good." Rafi smiled wisely and warmly. The kid's voice was so sweet, Mike felt like it was healing the burnt skin on the back of his neck just to hear it.

But behind Rafael stood someone else. Scalp askew, scarred and bleeding, his grudge open on his face, he could have been Rafael's bigger, terrifying, evil twin.

Chuy.

"Bullshit, *cabrón*," Chuy sneered. "You're going to Hell, and when you get here, you're mine."

"What?" Mike stumbled.

"I know it," Chuy said, jerking his thumb at Rafael, "*he* knows it, and *you* know it."

And Mike *did* know it.

"I'm sorry, Chuy," he said. He felt tears on his cheeks. "I was wrong."

Chuy spat blood onto the stone. "*Vete a la chingada.*"

"Mike," pleaded the Angel Rafael. The voice pulled sweetly on Mike's heart.

"Shut up, bitch," Mike mumbled, and he thumbed the shock button on the taser.

Chatta-chatta-chatta.

Then the garden was gone, and Chuy was gone, and the kid Rafi—the archangel Raphael—lay on the super-kiva's platform, jerking spastically again. Mike released the shock button, knees buckling. He shook his head to clear the smell of flowers out of his brain and turned to check in on Adrian—

who lay unconscious on the ground, face-down in the middle of his chalk diagrams.

"Fundillo!" Mike shouted.

He grabbed Adrian and shook him. Pinched. Kicked. Slapped in the face. The buzzing of flies filled his ears, and Rafi groaned.

"Adrian!" he yelled into the wizard's ear.

Adrian snored.

Eddie and Jim backed up the side of the super-kiva. Eddie's shotgun hung at his side and he swung his fists at the Zvuvim, while Jim still slashed and poked. The big man moved like an acrobat, dodging blows by rolling to one side or the other, or leaping into the air and somersaulting over them. Eddie was surprisingly quick, too—he looked like he was using karate on the demon-flies, knifing them aside with the blades of his hand in short, economical motions—but they were still backing up, and getting close to the top of the platform.

On the other side, Twitch retreated, too. She was in human— human-like fairy, anyway—form and her movements looked slower than usual. She was bleeding, and she swung her two batons to keep the Baal at bay, as it lumbered and crashed its way up the side of the pyramid.

"Adrian!" Eddie yelled.

"Adrian!" Mike yelled.

Adrian snored.

Rafi stirred and groaned.

"Cojón," Mike grumbled, but he had an idea. His heart raced and his head swam from the adrenalin, but he remembered that his clip was empty. He managed to switch out the old clip and slap in the

full one without dropping either, and then he placed the muzzle of his pistol against Adrian's buttock.

And squeezed the trigger.

Bang!

Blood gushed out onto the diagrams, and Adrian shook awake.

"Ouch!" the wizard roared. "Hey!"

Mike stared at the blood. "I thought …" he said. "You said it didn't break the skin … wards of shields, or something. …"

"Moron!" Adrian roared, and stumbled to his feet. He clutched his backside with one hand, blood welling out between his fingers. "The wards wear off!"

"Well, you're awake, anyway," Mike muttered.

Raphael groaned and twitched. For good measure, and because he felt embarrassed and didn't know what else to do, Mike shocked the angel again, and this time held down the button good and long.

Chatta-chatta-chatta-chatta-chatta-zotzpf!

The taser died in his hand, a shower of sparks scorching Mike's skin.

"Oh, Hell," Adrian said, and whipped his lens to his eye to look at the platform again. Holding his own butt and squinting through what amounted to a monocle made him look almost silly, and Mike started to laugh out loud.

"Is it wrecked?" Mike asked over the roaring of the Hound and the bellowing of the Baal Zavuv, both drawing closer up the sides of the super-kiva.

"I never yet saw a spell ruined by the addition of human blood," Adrian growled, putting away his lens. "Including this one. Stand back."

Mike stepped back, standing at the edge of the platform beside the unconscious boy-angel and pointing his pistol at Rafi, just in case. Rafi stirred, slightly. Eddie and Twitch both backed to within a step or two of the height of the pyramid, batting at the beasts that pursued them and the Zvuvim overhead. Mike was afraid to take his pistol off the prone angel, so he swung when he could with his fist at the fly-demons, batting them away without doing any real damage.

"*In Wepwawet nomini,*" Adrian shouted dramatically, despite his funny gimp posture, with all his weight on one leg, one hand waving in the air and the other clutching his own wounded buttock, "*aperiri te mando!*"

The flat space atop the kiva, with all Adrian's chalk markings on it, disappeared. A pit yawned beneath Mike's feet.

CHAPTER NINE

Mike teetered on the edge of the pit, unsure what the others would do. He had expected to see stairs down, and the gaping hole caught him totally by surprise. He flapped his arms like that would keep him in the air and looked for handholds or a rope or anything. He didn't find any, but in his flailing he knocked away the flashlight.

Adrian didn't hesitate. The wizard stepped forward and threw himself into the pit and the darkness. Probably had wards of bouncing, or something crazy like that on him, Mike thought, but the bellowing Baal and roaring Hound and the buzzing Zvuvim left him no choice, and he jumped in right after, clenching his teeth hard so he didn't scream.

He fell—

a beam of light tumbled in after him, spinning around—

looking up, hands pawing at the air, through the square of dimmer darkness above him, glimmering with multicolored flames, he saw shapes pass—

bodies falling—

Splash!

Water closed over Mike's head. So cold, Mike couldn't imagine why it wasn't ice. He fought for air and sucked in water instead, coughing and choking and flailing to get out. He sank, and in the dark water around him he felt other objects hitting the surface and thrashing about, and then beams of light from Eddie's Maglite cut the darkness, and finally, lungs searing with pain, Mike tried to swim.

He wasn't a very good swimmer, had always lived in desert country and had never been a gym rat, but he managed to fight to the surface. He coughed out cold fluid, feeling like a piece of his lung went with it, and kept fighting his way forward. Fists and feet thrashing in the darkness hit his shoulders and back and he tried to ignore them. Someone screamed wordlessly, a sound that echoed huge in the dark space. Mike worried that it might have been him.

After a few long strokes, Mike's hands slapped against something that felt like a brick wall, and he clung to it.

He'd lost the pistol, he realized, somewhere in the pool. *Chingado.* He groaned with effort and dragged himself out of the water. He heard the sloshing sounds of others doing the same, and lots of gasping for air. Mike was dimly aware that overhead, somewhere, danced the strange colored fire of the Hellhound. For some reason, it wasn't diving in right after them.

But it didn't sound very happy, either.

In the dark, he heard puffing breath and muttered curses, and then Eddie shone his light around and Mike could make out a little better what was going on.

The chamber was a cube of mud brick. In the center of the floor was a round sunken pool, and to one side, lying on the ground, was a pole-ladder like the one Mike had ruined outside. Water flowed into the pool through a brick channel from one wall, and flowed out the other. Eddie and Adrian crowded over the channel and looked closely at it. Teeth chattered, breath steamed and drops of water hit the floor off all their bodies while the guitar and organ players examined the sluice, and Twitch flapped in the air above them in falcon form

Above, Mike saw the flame of the Hellhound's body as it shoved its neck into the hole at the top of the super-kiva. It didn't seem to be able to fit, and as it jammed its head into the opening, it shouldered out the Baal. The fly-demon bellowed and squealed in irritation, and the Hound barked and screeched in return. The Baal's minions, the Zvuvim, crowded in through the hole and buzzed in a cloud below it, but didn't descend. Something was stopping all of them from jumping down in the hole after their quarry. Mike cringed at their noises and wondered what was saving his life; whatever it was, he was grateful for it.

"Isn't that just Hebrew?" Eddie sounded puzzled.

"Guys," Mike's teeth rattled in his head as he shivered. "Whatever you're doing, can you hurry?"

Twitch dropped out of her bird form and stood beside the other two. It looked like stretching downward, the falcon's legs growing longer and longer until suddenly the drummer stood there in person. The only thing that didn't shift or change in the process was Twitch's silvery horse's tail.

Mike blinked.

"It's the names of God," Adrian said. "Very old warding, very powerful. The water flows over all the names of God and into the cistern…. Hey! My butt!" The wizard slapped his own backside and Eddie shone the light on it. "No wound!"

It was true; through the hole he'd blasted in the organ player's pants, Mike could see the guy's buttock. No wound, no blood.

Mike felt goose pimples on his arms that had nothing to do with the cold, and he probed the back of his own neck. It didn't hurt, and the skin under his fingers felt soft and new, more like a baby's skin than his own coarse, hairy body.

"Holy water!" Mike blurted. He remembered enough about church to remember holy water. "The names of God must turn it into some kind of holy water. You know, like for healing, I guess. And good against vampires." He trailed off, unsure whether or not he was sounding like an idiot.

"And evil spirits," said a voice in the darkness.

Eddie whipped around and shone his light on the source of the sound. Rafael stood on the other side of the cistern.

"Don't let him talk!" Mike shouted.

"Don't worry, big guy," Adrian reassured him. "Twitch isn't susceptible to the Whisper of Eden. Neither is Jim. If this bastard tries anything, he goes down."

"Maybe I should kill him anyway," Eddie growled, and Mike heard the emphatic *snicker* of a shell being popped into the underside of the shotgun. "Why aren't you wet, you rotten weasel?"

It was true, Mike realized. Rafi was dry as a bone. Twitch was too, but of course Twitch could fly. "This is the pool where the leader of the rebels was imprisoned," Rafi said, ignoring Eddie and pointing at the water. "Of course you know that, it's why you're here. The water was sanctified, and it held him down. Paralyzed by the pain."

Mike scratched his head. The same water that had healed him had kept Satan imprisoned, because it *hurt* the fallen angel? What kind of holy water *was* that?

"What happened?" Adrian asked warily. "He got out eventually, so what was it? Did one of the names erode off? But that can't be it, can it, or the water would be ordinary mundane liquid now."

Rafi nodded. "There was a drought," he said. "When the water got low enough, Azazel managed to kick his way out."

"That's when he chipped his hoof," Adrian concluded. "Guess he was so excited to get out, he didn't notice."

Rafi shrugged. "Or he hurt too much."

Eddie guffawed his derision. "It figures you'd build a prison that depended on water in the *desert*."

Rafi smiled. "There was water enough," he said. "Until the flood. But when the fountains of the great deep spat forth their waters to obliterate the wickedness of the children of men in the days of Noah, the rock seep dried up."

"And in forty days, the prison evaporated." Adrian shook his head. "Serves you right, you idiots."

The demons above raged.

Mike's head whirled among astonishment and curiosity and disbelief and fear, like the spinner of an old Snakes and Ladders game, whizzing in circles while all the players watched to see how many spaces Mikey would get to go, and whether he'd step on the bottom of a ladder or the top of a snake. Mike felt like there were snakes all around him, and no ladders anywhere in sight. He pawed at the cluster of holy amulets on his chest, but they didn't help.

"What do you want, Raphael? You can't talk us out of anything." Eddie's voice had a hard, flat edge to it, and it snapped Mike back into focus on the here and now. "And I have the gun."

"I want to deal," Rafi said. "I want to be on the team."

"No way," Eddie shot back. "I don't make bargains with supernatural forces."

"Once burned," Adrian added, "you know the rest."

"Besides," Twitch threw in, "what do you have to offer us? We're here. We beat you."

"Did you?" Rafael smiled. "Where's the hoof, then? Where's your escape route? Those demons can smell the water and don't want to fall into it, but sooner or later they'll find another way in, or they'll get desperate enough to become reckless and jump anyway. And if they don't, you're stuck here forever. What's your plan to deal with them? And where's Jim?"

The Hound howled bitterly.

Mike realized he *hadn't* seen Jim inside the pyramid—the singer's silence and the darkness had made him forget the man. Eddie spun around, shining his light until he found a wet mass by the side of the cistern, trembling in silence.

"I don't think falling into the water was a very pleasant experience for Jim," Rafi said. "His father certainly didn't like it."

"His father?" Pieces clicked into place for Mike. The rapid pace of events around him had kept him from making all the connections, but now he saw it. "Of course. Jim is Azazel's son."

"Poor bastard." Eddie handed the shotgun to Adrian, knelt by Jim and shook him. "Jim, are you awake?"

Adrian shone the light around the room and scrutinized its walls and ceiling. "Don't get any ideas, angel," he said coldly. "We still have the fairy, and he knows how to bite."

"Where's the hoof, though?" Twitch wondered.

"I needed you," Rafael said. "I have been the keeper of this prison for six thousand years, but I have never known how to open it. I wasn't given any key, wasn't told how. That was deliberate policy, of course, on the part of Heaven. They couldn't have me developing sympathies and betraying my trust."

"Yeah, I know that's what *I* immediately think of when I hear the word *angel*," Adrian muttered. "How *sympathetic* you guys are."

Mike remembered Rafi almost yanking his arm from his socket as he threw him sideways and stole his gun. "Amen," he muttered.

"I needed you to open the crypt. And now I could just take the hoof and go, but I want to join you. I want to aid you in your quest."

"Bullshit," Eddie disagreed. "Who do you think I am, Sir Lancelot? You don't care about my *quest* one way or the other, anyhow, you lying sack. You have your own game."

"Fine," Rafi admitted. "I have my own game. But we can play our games at the same time. I'll tell you where the hoof is, we defeat the Hound and the bugs together, and then we go put the hoof to good use."

"I don't want to put it to *good* use," Adrian said. "A leopard can't change, et cetera."

"Bad use, then!" Rafi snapped.

And then Mike knew where the hoof was.

"He can't get it," he told Adrian. "Rafi—*Raphael* can't get the hoof. He's frustrated. He still needs us."

"Of course he can't get it," Eddie agreed. He was helping Jim to a sitting position. Jim groaned. Adrian shone the light on the singer and he looked pink, like someone had thrown boiling water on him. "Or he wouldn't be bargaining. But where is it?"

"It's like he said," Adrian added. "Heaven didn't want him to grab the hoof, either." He turned on the angel, shining the light on him and stalking closer. "What is it you want, Raphael? Freedom? Do you just want to lay your calling down and go? Power? Are you hoping you can bargain your way into the Infernal Council? Or maybe get a promotion in Heaven? Who outranks the archangels? The seraphim? Is that it, you want to be one of Heaven's six-winged pool-boys, basking forever in the golden light of the throne?"

"Do you care?" Anger flashed in Rafi's eyes. "Does it matter to you?"

"It matters!" Adrian snapped. "I have plans for that hoof!"

"What do you want?" Rafi asked. "You want to be a real wizard, don't you? You want to cast the big spells, and you don't want to fall asleep when you do it. And Eddie there wants to save his soul. Jim, I can guess. You're like Dorothy and her friends, on a twisted road to Oz to see the wizard. And you're going to trade the wizard his hoof in return for brains and courage and a heart and a return ticket home."

"I guess you get TV reception in Dudael," Adrian chuckled.

"I can get what I want from Azazel," Rafi said firmly. "And I can help you all get what you want."

"No deal," Eddie's voice was flat. He pushed Jim to his feet, his shoulder under the big man's arm. Jim was groggy, and slow to respond. "Not now, not ever."

"We already have someone who can talk us out of traffic tickets," Adrian sneered. "You just don't bring anything to the table."

"I'll tell," the kid said. He sounded petulant, and since the moment when he'd stolen Mike's gun and thrown him off the kiva, he'd never looked more like a little kid.

"Azazel?" Eddie snorted. "We'll tell him ourselves."

"I'll tell Heaven."

"Tell them what, exactly?" Adrian shone the flashlight into Rafi's eyes, and the angel held up his hands to block the beam. "Tell them you went behind their back and tried to cut some kind of deal with Hell?"

Rafi laughed. "Of course not! I'll tell them how you overpowered me and stole the hoof, and where you're headed. And then I'll laugh as Heaven's pool-boys chop you to pieces with their flaming swords."

"Aren't you afraid Heaven can hear you now?" Adrian asked.

"Of course not!" Rafi laughed. "Do you think Heaven wanted Azazel to be able to just call for his friends, and be rescued? This place is warded to silence so deep, nothing can get out. You could set off a nuclear bomb in here, and no one would hear. The screaming of a thousand damned souls wouldn't get past the roof."

Adrian pulled something from his pocket and held it over his head. It looked like a smartphone. *Click*, Mike heard, and then Rafi's voice repeated, *I'll laugh as Heaven's pool-boys chop you to pieces with their flaming swords.*

"You recorded me?" Rafi sounded incredulous.

"There's an app for that," Adrian sneered.

"But …"

"Don't mess with the gadget guy, bitch!" Adrian spat. The kid stepped back and his face twisted into an expression of anger and fear. "Now stay out of the way, or you'll be the one with his nuts on Heaven's anvil!"

"That doesn't solve our basic problem," Eddie observed. "It's funny as hell, of course, but we still don't know where the hoof is. If it's even here at all."

The Hound howled at them above, as if to emphasize the point. Mike felt goose pimples on his arms and he couldn't wait any longer.

"Isn't it obvious?" he asked, and jumped into the pool.

He wasn't a very good swimmer, and as he thrashed his way to the bottom of the pool, grabbing handfuls of water and pushing them up, exhaling and trying to sink his own weight and wishing he were a little thinner, he wondered what he was doing. He didn't know how deep the water was, he didn't know what might be at the bottom, and he wasn't really sure he wanted to be further pissing off the archangel Raphael, who was already probably irritated at the repeated tasering Mike had given him.

Plus, he couldn't really be sure he was right about where the hoof was.

But he wanted to take a stand. He wanted to show his worth to the team, and he wanted to be part of something. He wasn't afraid of the water, however bad a swimmer he was—it seemed to have healed his burns, and that made him feel that it wouldn't drown him, either. Totally irrational, but that's what he felt in his gut. Besides, maybe, whatever the band was planning to do with the hoof, it could also be used to help him with Chuy. It sounded like they were going to go bargain with the devil. Well, if the devil could make Adrian a real wizard and give Twitch a brain, or whatever it was she wanted, maybe he could set Chuy free, too.

And that might free Mike.

He hit the pool bottom and almost immediately found the hoof.

It was huge, as long as Mike's forearm and curved like a scythe. For a moment he thought it must not be what he was looking for, but Adrian was shining down the light from above now, and Mike could see the bottom of the pool—it wasn't very big, and there wasn't anything else. Besides, the thing he'd found felt like a hoof, like a gigantic discarded nail clipping. He grabbed it in both hands.

Then he saw his pistol. No sense going unarmed, not in all this craziness.

Mike scooped up the gun, jammed it into his belt and kicked off for the surface.

He surfaced from the water, shaking himself like a dog. The first thing he saw when he opened his eyes was a shattered heap of plastic and wire on the brick beside the pool. It was Adrian's smartphone, he realized, stomped into fragments. Looking up, he found Adrian standing in the beam of the flashlight with his hands over his head.

"Who's got the gun?" he asked, and then he saw Twitch behind Adrian, blood on her mouth like she'd been hit. Jim and Eddie stood behind the drummer, the singer still leaning heavily on his guitar player for support. "Oh," he said.

"Slight miscalculation," Twitch told him with a wry shrug.

"I got cocky," Adrian grumbled. "Should have given the gun to the fairy."

"Thank you, Mike," Rafi said. He sounded polite and amused. "Go ahead and bring me the hoof."

"Don't do it!" Adrian snapped, but Rafi's voice was warm and pleasant and anyway, Rafi was Mike's friend. Mike dragged his soggy carcass out of the water. He belly-flopped onto the soft green grass like a beached whale, but his friends wouldn't care, and besides, the sun was warm and the breeze was gentle. He smiled as he handed the gigantic toenail clipping over to his friend Rafael.

"Good job, Mike," the boy grinned, and took the hoof.

"Hell," Eddie said. Poor Eddie, he was always so grumpy, Mike thought. Even when the weather was perfect, like this.

"Not Hell," Rafi said, "Eden. Now, Mike, would you please go get that ladder and set it up? There are some friends I'd like to join us."

"Of course." Mike found the ladder on the green sward and grunted as he tried to pick it up. "It's kind of heavy."

"Adrian," Rafi suggested. "Would you mind helping?"

"Not at all." Adrian and Mike together picked up the ladder and hoisted it up against the ceiling. Except there was no ceiling, there was only blue sky above. Mike's brain skipped like a vinyl record with a scratch on that thought. There was blue sky above, but he had just placed a ladder up into an opening in the sky. Something didn't quite click, and he felt his brain skipping again.

Far away, maybe in the forest over the hill, some big creature made its presence known with a shriek that thundered through the trees and sounded like it would uproot them all by sheer sonic power. It might be a Tyrannosaurus Rex, Mike thought.

"Calling for your father won't help," Rafi said pleasantly. He was talking to Jim, who looked tired and haggard despite the pleasant surroundings, and leaned on Eddie for support. "Assuming you'd want to. But maybe you can play with his servants." Mike heard the buzzing of flies, a small blight on the beauty of the day.

"Jim!" Eddie snapped.

"Phthonos!" Jim shouted, and suddenly the illusion of the garden and the forest and the sunshine and the distant sea snapped to shards like a stained glass window with a brick thrown through it. Jim's voice echoed deep and strong—it *did* have reverb in it naturally, Mike would have sworn—and the inside of the super-kiva returned to view.

But who was Jim yelling at?

The Hound jammed its head through the opening at the top of the pyramid and howled. Jets of blue and red fire crackled from its rows of jagged teeth, lighting the interior like a carnival funhouse ride.

Was Jim calling the Hellhound?

"Jeez," Mike muttered. He felt sick.

The archangel Raphael stood in the corner of the kiva, shotgun in his hands. The pyramid began to fill with Zvuvim and smaller flies, buzzing incessantly in a cloud of clacketing steel and black fly-demon flesh that descended out of the ceiling. The stink of rotting meat choked the air inside the chamber.

Inside the cloud, rattling down the ladder one heavy step at a time and shaking dust as it came, the Baal Zavuv descended into the kiva.

"Phthonos!" Jim shouted again, and something in the big man's voice heartened Mike without any apparent intent to do so. "Attack!"

Chapter Ten

Mike charged.

He jerked the pistol from the back of his belt and drew a bead on the archangel Raphael, squeezing the trigger.

Click.

"Huevos!" Mike cursed.

Boom!

He saw the muzzle flash of the shotgun and thought he'd bought the farm, but Rafi wasn't shooting at him. Eddie and Jim tumbled to the ground together, and then Mike crashed on top of the archangel in the body of the little boy.

He raised his fist over his head and clubbed Rafi over the ear with the pistol's grip.

"Ouch!" The kid staggered under the blow.

Mike saw in his mind's eye what would happen next. The angel would blow him to bits with the shotgun, unless he managed to stop it. So he dropped his pistol and threw himself on the bigger gun, wrestling for control.

Buzzzzzz.

A knife sank into his back and then another, and Mike screamed in agony. He felt the legs of the Zavuv on his back and legs and smelled the dry-dust stink of the fly-demon, but he couldn't let it stop him. He grabbed the barrel of the shotgun and threw his weight against it, trying to fall and rip it bodily from the angel's hands.

Boom!

The gun went off, and Mike wasn't dead.

"Get off!"

Rafi backhanded Mike across the face and hurled him across the room—

Buzzzzz! a second Zavuv intercepted Mike in midair, sinking its mandibles into his chest—

Mike screamed again—

"Per Volcanum—" Adrian shouted, and then Rafi clubbed him in the face with the shotgun and he fell like a sack of grain—

Mike landed in the cistern of holy water.

The Zvuvim on his body exploded into flame and he sank, fire burning him before and behind, and at the same time feeling the delicious ice-cool soothing touch of the waters. This was some kind of insanity, Mike thought. Feeling two opposite things at the same time, like loving and hating someone.

Though as he thought of it, he realized that's how he felt about Chuy.

Which, of course, might be madness.

At the bottom of the pool, the smoldering flies fell away from him and he bounced back toward the surface. Mike emerged from the water feeling refreshed and whole.

ROAR—CRACK!

The Hellhound smashed its shoulders against the entrance in the ceiling, knocking loose bricks and dust that fell and peppered the water around Mike. Eddie and Adrian both lay prone and still, and Jim fought the Baal Zavuv.

Jim was a wild man, like a monkey or a comic book character. As Mike stared, Jim ran up the corner of the room like it was a flat surface, dodging a swipe of the Baal's enormous claw. From over the Baal's head, Jim kicked off and flipped backwards through the air, landing with both heels on the Baal's shoulders. The Baal raged and swiped, but Jim dodged, moving from one foot to the other with casual grace, batting and slashing aside dive-bombing Zvuvim all the while.

His balance and speed were inhuman, Mike thought.

Because, of course, Jim *wasn't* human. Jim was the son of Satan.

Twitch dashed around the Baal, landing blows on it as she could with her wooden batons, but mostly smashing Zvuvim to the ground, keeping them off Eddie's and Adrian's bodies.

The archangel Raphael stood back in the corner of the room, holding the shotgun and the hoof of the rebel Azazel and laughing his head off.

"Phthonos!" Jim yelled again.

The Hound answered him with a long, loud hollering cry that was almost mournful.

Mike shook himself. He needed to act.

Adrian was closer. Mike crept forward, hoping that the spectacle would distract Rafael until he could grab the organ player's leg. Fortunately, Adrian was a small man. Mike wrapped his fingers around the wizard's ankle and pulled, dragging the little man into the pool.

As they both splashed into the water, Adrian started thrashing around. Mike grabbed the wizard by the collar of his jacket and pushed off the floor, bringing them both up to good breathable air again—

and staring into the open mouth of the shotgun.

"You've been a lot of trouble, Mike," the archangel Raphael snarled through the mouth of the little kid. "Time to say good-bye."

He pumped the shotgun, pointed it at Mike's head and squeezed the trigger—

Boom!—

Mike threw himself back into the water—

he felt the shotgun slug tear into his chest and felt the flesh healing up behind the projectile immediately, his whole body tingling like electricity.

Boom! He heard another shot while he was underwater, muffled, and felt another slug hit him in the hip. He felt the bone break, and felt it knit again, almost instantly.

Mike came up again spluttering, ecstatic and totally disoriented. Jim and Twitch fought the Baal and its Zvuvim in the background, the flies swarming around them like a curtain, opaque and buzzing.

"Damn you!" Raphael shouted. "Get out of the water!"

"No!" the shout came from Eddie, who had struggled to his feet. Blood ran down his chest from a hole in his shirt and he looked worn and broken, but he broke into a charge. *"You* get *in!"*

Eddie rammed the kid with his shoulder and wrapped both arms around him, launching both of them into the air—

out over the pool—

and *splash!* into the water.

Rafi hit the water and lit up like an incandescent bulb. Light seemed to burn inside him and rocketed from the entire surface of his body as he and Eddie sank. He looked like a living X-ray image—Mike thought he could see bones glowing through his skin, flailing and trembling as he sank. Mike grabbed for Eddie and was nearly blinded by the glow of the kid beside him. He managed to dig his fingers into the guitar player's army jacket and drag the man up, out of the water.

The light streamed up, out of Rafi's body like a bolt of lightning in reverse, a column that shot straight for heaven, through the open top of the pyramid and into the stone overhang above it, and then was gone.

Rafi thrashed as the light left him, then went limp. Adrian grabbed the boy, hauling him up, and Eddie—looking much healthier and moving better—got himself upright. Eddie ducked under the water again and grabbed his shotgun; Mike picked up the crescent of hoof-clipping, floating on the surface, and the three of them moved toward the edge of the pool and the cloud of Zvuvim surrounding Jim and Twitch.

Eddie rested his elbow on the edge of the pool. He pumped the shotgun, aimed into the cloud and squeezed the trigger.

Click.

"I guess it's knives, boys," Eddie muttered darkly. "Unless one of you has that escape plan Raphael was blabbering about." He started dragging himself out of the water.

With a lightning-like backhand, the Baal finally landed a blow on Twitch, punching her with its enormous knuckles in her chest. Twitch hit the wall and sank to the floor in a spray of bright blood. Zvuvim swarmed her.

Mike and Adrian dragged themselves out on Eddie's heels. Adrian was already muttering something. Mike dug into his pocket for a weapon and came up with nothing but a pocketknife.

"Phthonos!" Jim yelled again, his huge voice barely audible under the carpet of swarming Zvuvim. Mike thought he saw the singer, sword in one hand and a pinned Zavuv in the other, parrying attacking fly-demons with the body of their comrade and stabbing at the face of the Baal Zavuv. He looked bloody and tired.

ROAAAR—CRASH!!

With a final lunge, the Hellhound broke through the ceiling. It fell in a shower of bricks and flame straight toward the pool, and Mike scrambled to get out of its way. Adrian didn't move—he struggled to incant something, heaving his chest and shaking his head like he was fighting to stay awake.

Krakkkksh!

The Hellhound landed on the edge of the cistern, its front paws and head out of the water, and its hind legs and tail landing in. It missed Adrian by scant feet, and the wizard stumbled sideways from the shock. Steam gusted up from where the water doused the Hound's flames on contact.

The Hound shrieked and snarled in furious pain.

Grrrraaaaaraaargh! the Baal bellowed in answer.

Jim leaned against the wall. He'd been hit by something, and didn't seem to be able to stand on his own anymore. The Baal towered over him, claws lashing like bandsaws and tusks gnashing at the air.

"Per Isidem—" Adrian collapsed to the floor.

Mike snapped open the puny blade and followed Eddie, charging at the pile of Zvuvim crawling over Twitch. It's over, he thought. This is where I die.

I hope Chuy's not waiting for me on the other side.

He stabbed his little knife into the nearest fly-demon, waiting for his own destruction.

The Hellhound lunged forward, roaring—

and clamped its enormous crocodilian jaws around the waist of the Baal Zavuv.

The Baal howled in fury and surprise. The Hound lifted it off the ground and shook it. Zvuvim buzzed around the two larger demons, whining in to slash with their mandibles at the Hellhound and bursting into flame on contact.

Zvuvim stampeded away from Twitch, nearly knocking Mike over as they buffeted into and past him. The drummer was left in a heap on the floor.

"Twitch," Eddie and Mike said together.

She raised a hand weakly and grinned. "Not dead yet."

"Let's get you into the pool," Mike suggested, and stooped to pick her up.

Twitch slapped away his hands, suddenly animated. "Whoa, Mike, not me! I've seen what happens to immortals who get into that water!"

"Immortals?" Mike scratched his head. "Uh, of course." There was no *of course* about it, though. He had a lot to learn, and he knew it.

Mike turned back to the battle that raged between the two demons. The Hound rushed at the wall of the chamber—

the Baal sank its claws into the Hellhound's shoulder—

"Attack, Phthonos!" Jim yelled—

and the Hound slammed the Baal into the wall, head-first.

CRACK!

Grwaaaaargh!

Blue sparks crackled at the point of impact. Zvuvim swarmed the Hound with angry, frenetic buzzing, which was almost enough to make Mike feel sorry for the beast. When they struck its front half, which still flamed, they burnt and died, but when they attacked its hindquarters they drew blood. The Hound swung about, obviously in pain, managing to stomp on a few of the flies or catch them with its flaming forepaws.

Meanwhile, the Baal Zavuv clawed at the Hound's head. The Baal's flesh smoked and scorched and stank, and with an enraged bellow it tore off one of the Hound's ears.

"Attack!" Jim yelled again.

The Hound charged at the wall again, swinging its head to slam the Baal's skull against the brick. One of the Baal's eyes shattered on impact, spraying thick ichor on the wall and floor in another shower of fizzing blue sparks. The Baal shrieked and sank all its talons into the head and neck of the Hellhound.

Mike noticed the gray pallor of pre-dawn early morning creeping in through the opening at the top of the pyramid. He almost chuckled.

"Attack!"

The Zvuvim swarmed the Hound so thickly Mike couldn't even see its flames anymore, and the inside of the super-kiva was shrouded in thick shadow. The Hellhound charged the wall and smashed the Baal into it a final time—

CRACK!

The wall collapsed.

Brick dust, bricks, and ancient timbers hidden inside the walls exploded in a spray of masonry chaos and waves of blue fire over the struggling demons. Mike staggered back, pulling Twitch with him away from the wall, which continued to tumble, one brick at a time, each brick exploding in blue sparks as it hit the floor. Finally Mike found the corner, coughing and spitting dust on the floor and wiping muddy grit from his eyes.

And then there was silence.

"Twitch?" Mike called. "Eddie?"

He was rewarded with an answering cough. "I'm here," he heard. It was Eddie's voice. "I've got Adrian. He's alive."

"I'm alive, too," Mike heard Twitch say from somewhere very close, and then realized he was clutching her to himself like a scared kid would hold a rag doll. And she felt like a man.

"Uh, sorry," Mike said, feeling awkward.

"Sorry you saved me?" Twitch asked.

"No," Mike answered immediately. He stood, and helped Twitch stand, too. "Sorry, I … uh, I don't know. I don't know anything. Sorry."

Twitch laughed. "Welcome to the band," the drummer said, and kissed him on the cheek.

Mike chose to think of Twitch as a woman, and to enjoy the kiss.

Splash!

The dust was settling enough that Mike could see Eddie dragging Adrian into the pool. When the wizard hit the water he woke up, spitting and cursing.

Then he found Rafi. The boy lay under a fur of brick dust, breathing deeply like he was sound asleep.

"What about Jim?" Mike asked. He approached the pile of rubble, finding himself standing in the weak light of morning among the bodies of what seemed like a hundred giant flies. He could see the tail and back legs of the Hellhound sticking out from under the bricks. There were no flames, and he wondered if the creature was dead.

And then the tail swished.

"Help!" Mike snapped, and jumped back.

But then Jim was there, patting the big creature on its rump and talking to it. "Easy, Phthonos," Jim said in his strange, booming voice. "Easy. Friends."

The Hound shook its big flaming crocodile head free of the rubble, dropping the torn and broken body of the Baal Zavuv into the dust. The front half of its body still burned, and as Mike watched, smoke began to rise from its hindquarters as well.

"You're talking," Mike said.

"Wards of silence," Jim grinned. He was dusty and bloody and his t-shirt was destroyed, but he looked totally unconquerable. Then his grin fell off and he yelled to Adrian. "Please tell me there really are wards of silence in here, and they're still intact."

Adrian rinsed off his lens in the cistern's water and squinted through it at the chamber around him. "Yeah," he said, "it's all still there. But it's starting to fall apart, so you'd better shut up and we'd better get moving. A stitch in time, you know."

"Stay," Jim said to the Hellhound. It made a loud rumbling sound in its belly that sounded like the purr of an oversized lion. "Stay, Phthonos."

"The Hound obeys you," Mike said. He felt numb, and wondered if he was going into shock.

"Some of my father's minions are too stupid to know any better," Jim nodded. "And some have divided loyalties. That's the problem with Hell."

"I don't know," Mike shook his head, thinking of Raphael. "It seems to be a problem with Heaven, too."

"Maybe it's a problem with thinking creatures generally," Jim agreed. "Or maybe it's not a *problem* at all. Maybe it's just the effect of free will. Will you join us?" He stood and held out his hand.

Mike cleared his throat; he wanted to sound professional. "How many dates on the tour?" he asked.

"I don't know."

"Where are we going?"

"I don't know. Probably Chicago, for one."

Mike nodded down at the Hound, purring at Jim's feet. "Are we going to meet more friends like this one?"

"Almost certainly."

Mike thought of his flophouse room in Santa Fe. He thought of Chuy, too, and then he shook Jim's hand. "Sounds like a real crappy gig," he laughed, a little bitterly. "But the alternative is worse."

"That's how I make most of my decisions." Jim smiled. "Phthonos, stay," he repeated, and then he took the hoof from Mike's hands and walked out of the crumbling super-kiva through the hole in its wall. The Hellhound stayed behind.

Freakishly, it wagged its tail.

Twitch followed right behind Jim, in her horse shape, with the boy Rafi slung over her back. Adrian walked next to her, holding the kid in place. He patted Mike on the shoulder as he passed. "Good to have a rhythm section again," he said.

Eddie brought up the rear. "Can you drive?" he asked.

Mike nodded. "I've been a driver before."

"Cab, or limo?"

Mike sighed. "Getaway car, mostly," he admitted.

"Perfect," Eddie laughed.

"I had a rough youth."

"Everybody does. Let's go get the instruments and hit the road, before Fido here remembers that daddy sent it to fetch Jim."

Mike scratched his head and they both walked out of the kiva. Mike shot one last look over his shoulder at the Hellhound, and was rewarded with a lopsided crocodilian grin. A fresh, water-bearing breeze blew into the overhang from the canyon below, and he breathed deep. "Aren't they burnt to cinders?" he asked.

"All the band gear is fireproof and impact-resistant," Eddie told him.

"Wards of instrument insurance?"

Eddie chuckled. "Something like that. Your bass is probably gone, but we have another one you can use."

"I saw it in the van," Mike remembered. "I'll try not to impale myself on it."

"That'd be good," Eddie agreed. "That'd be a real good start."

About The Author

D.J. Butler (Dave) is a novelist living in the Rocky Mountain northwest. His training is in law, and he worked as a securities lawyer at a major international firm and inhouse at two multinational semiconductor manufacturers before taking up writing fiction. He is a lover of language and languages, a guitarist and self-recorder, and a serious reader. He is married to a powerful and clever woman and together they have three devious children.

Dave has been writing fiction since 2010. He writes speculative fiction (roughly, fantasy, science fiction, space opera, steampunk, cyberpunk, superhero, alternate history, dystopian fiction, horror and related genres) for all audiences. He has written and is writing novels for middle grade, young adult and adult readers. He is working on getting published via the traditional route; in the meantime, he is entertaining readers with Rock Band Fights Evil. Dave has always had a soft spot for good pulp fiction.

Follow the band at:

http://rockbandfightsevil.com.

Read about D.J. Butler's other writing projects at:

http://davidjohnbutler.com.

Other WordFire Press Titles by D.J. Butler

Rock Band Fights Evil:

Snake Handlin' Man

Crow Jane

Devil Sent the Rain

Crecheling

Our list of other WordFire Press authors and titles is always growing. To find out more and to see our selection of titles, visit us at:

wordfirepress.com